The Bell River Murder

The Bell River Murder

A Jenna Stack Mystery

Hanna Wren

ISBN: 979-8-9878098-5-3

Cover Design: Jessie Horsting

For all of the teachers, coaches, and mentors out there who make a difference every day.

Contents

Chapter 1
Home for the Holidays

The train shudders to a stop with a long wheezing sound. Bell River Station is on the wrong side of town by a stretch of barren earth locals call the Scrublands. The small brick depot is unmanned, butted up against a cement parking lot. Dark woods surround the isolated platform. The station is deserted on this gray afternoon. I expected more activity on Christmas Eve.

Only one other traveler, an older man wearing horn-rimmed glasses and earmuffs, is left on the train. All of the other passengers exited at more cheerful destinations farther south. Without making eye contact, he pops up from his seat, grabs his bag, and slips out. I text my mom.

Me: *Just arriving. Called an Uber. See you soon.*

I pull my roller bag from the overhead compartment and drag it onto the platform. The minute I step outside, my breath rushes out in a cloud. The cement is frosted with ice and slippery. But I know the drill. I grew up in this iceberg of a town. What do they say in Norway? "There is no bad weather, just bad clothing choices." I've packed an alluring wardrobe full of ski vests, gloves, mufflers, thermal shirts, and woolen socks, and I'm wearing my favorite lug-soled snow boots. Still, the cold in Bell River always surprises me.

Maybe it's the busy sidewalks, the steamy subway grates, or the rattling salt trucks, but ice never lasts long in New York City, where I live now. Here, ice creeps over everything, from the windows on the train to the bricks on the station building. Snowflakes swirl in the yellow lamplight. I can make out the river, cutting through the landscape, heavy with—you guessed it—more ice. I peek at the announcement board inside the station: 30 degrees. My fingers tingle as I zip my jacket tight.

An alarm chimes on my phone. My driver just arrived...somewhere out there.

Headlights blink on and off in the parking lot. I follow the beacon, dragging my suitcase behind. A small man jumps out of a Toyota 4Runner. He's wearing a plaid hunting cap, a heavy coat zipped up over his nose, and cheap-looking night vision glasses.

"Pick up for Jenna Stack."

"Over here." I wave even though we're alone.

He grabs my suitcase and opens up the back. "Remember me?"

I narrow my eyes in the dim light. "Um, I can't even see you."

The driver unzips the top of his jacket and grins. His broad face is rimmed by a scrubby beard peppered with gray hair. There's something about his eyes. They're mischievous. He certainly looks familiar, but...I shrug.

"Maybe this will help." He pulls a glowering expression. "Stay off that floor, kid; I just mopped."

"No! Mr. Barnes? The janitor?" I say, amazed.

"You're not a kid anymore. Call me Andy." He stomps his feet to stay warm.

"You always let me into school when I was late."

"And your brother, too. You were good kids, always polite, said hello. Not like those other rowdies." Andy loads my bag in the back of his SUV. "Climb in. I've got the heat running."

"My mom is staying at—"

"Annie Dupont's. I know. Moved in last year. Martha always did have the patience of a saint." Andy grins.

"Do you mind if I sit up front with you?"

"Riding shotgun, eh? Sure thing, city girl."

Andy pulls onto the snowy two-lane highway. After the congestion and tall buildings of New York, it's unsettling to see so much open space. We pass empty fields with dry stalks of grass poking up through the snow, then drive through the industrial section of town. Bad memories flood back. Mom, Tyler, and I had to move to a dingy two-bed apartment for a while when she was sick, and times were tough. I shake it off. Up ahead is the river, the dividing line between the Scrublands and the good side of town. The Winter Bridge stretches over a section of dark water choked with ice. A sloping hill leads to the water's edge, where the kids used to hang out...before the accident. Andy slows down as we pass by a metal plaque erected on the side of the road.

In Loving Memory of Abigail Wade.

Every town has its stories. In Bell River, everyone knows the story of little Abby Wade, who drowned in the river my senior year. A bunch of kids were skating by the Winter Bridge when the ice jam broke upstream. Abigail fell through the ice and was swept away to drown in the freezing water. When they announced her memorial service over the school sound system, every classroom erupted into whispers about how it happened and who was to blame.

"Poor Abby," I say. "She was such a sweet girl."

"Some folks think Abby Wade's death cursed Bell River, and it's just catching up with us now." Andy crosses himself.

Down the road, I see old brick buildings covered in twinkling lights. The town seems just as I remember...Until we get closer and I notice how many beautiful old homes look empty and neglected. Windows are boarded up with plywood, the curb is crumbling, and yards are dotted with foreclosure signs. Andy turns down Main Street. Every other shop is empty. All that's left is the grocery mart with gas pumps, a drug store, the police station, and a weather-beaten City Hall. The old movie theater is closed. Even the eagle statue in front of City Hall has been graffitied. The town is a rundown mess.

"My God, Andy. What's happened to this place?"

"I told you, something's not right. It started with just a few families leaving town. Then, the crime rate skyrocketed, and the real estate market crashed. It's starting to look like a ghost town. There's one new place, though. It's real nice. But not stuck up." He points ahead to the middle of the block. A cheerful red and white awning announcing Boomer's Bistro frames a large plate glass window lined with sparkling Christmas lights. I can make out a handful of figures seated in the cozy interior. The café looks totally out of place, and very appealing.

Then, I spot the billboard above City Hall plastered with a fresh ad. A man with red hair and a practiced smile faces the camera, his arm thrown around a petite blonde woman with perfect, doll-like features.

"Stop the car. Now!"

Andy slams the brakes. The four-wheeler slides on the icy street before coming to a stop. He looks at me like I've gone crazy.

"Is that—" I point at the sign.

"Woody Wade? Sure is."

The words Woody Wade for Congress are blazoned across the top of the sign.

"And Star Simonsen?" I'm shocked.

"Soon to be Mrs. Woody Wade, a real trophy wife, that one."

"Wait. Did you say they're engaged?" I can barely choke the words out.

"That's right."

I shake my head in disbelief. Star was my best friend in high school. I've been trying to reach her for the last month. Unlike the other popular girls, she was a total bookworm. We met at the library and bonded over detective novels. She was smart and independent, definitely not the trophy wife type.

"Woody claims he's going to fix this mess." Andy points at the neglected streets. "But I'm not so sure. That kid was a hellion. Remember when he almost burned the library down?"

"Sure do. One kid went to the hospital. That idiot is running for Congress?"

"Well, he is the son of the Sheriff," Andy reminds me as he accelerates slowly.

"I just remember him as the school bully," I point out.

And poor Abby Wade's brother. Even more shocking than Woody running for Congress is that Star Simonsen is engaged to the jerk. The image of the two of them together is unnerving. Clearly, a lot has changed. Why didn't Mom mention how bad things have gotten?

"Come on. Let's get you home." Andy takes a left and another right and pulls up in front of a rundown two-story duplex. The paint is peeling, and the porch stairs sag.

Cold air stings my eyes as I step out of the car. So this is where Mom is staying? It looks like a developer split these old houses down the middle and installed identical front doors side by side.

Andy wrestles my bag onto the sidewalk, puts a hand on my

shoulder, and looks me in the eye. "What happened with your brother ain't right. And your poor mother's had more than her share of grief. It's real nice you're here."

~

Annie Dupont is outside, bundled up in a puffer jacket with a striped scarf wrapped around her neck. She's wearing a knitted newsboy hat with a large daisy on the brim. Scattered around her are a bunch of seed pots. She digs up some crusted dirt and pops a seed in a pot before she trowels dirt over the top and methodically moves on to the next. Above her, icicles are frozen along the gutter. She addresses me before I can delicately ask her if she's lost her mind.

"So, you're back, are you?" Annie says without looking up.

"That's right, Mrs. Dupont. Isn't it a bit cold to be gardening?"

"I'm winter sowing." Annie straightens up, dusting dirt from her lap. "Germinating the seeds outside in the cold makes them stronger. That way, they're hardy and robust, used to the trials of being outside." She looks me up and down and frowns. "You look thinner than I remember."

"Well, I've been eating like a horse, so I'm not sure why."

"Maybe if you came home more often. What do you do in New York City anyway?"

Annie Dupont has always been a snob. Not only is she the lone real estate agent in town, but she's also the President of The Bell River Heritage Society. Somehow, whenever she opens her mouth, I feel like I'm being judged...probably because I am.

"Is Martha home?" I ignore her question.

Annie nods and motions to the adjoining townhouse.

"I'll never understand why you call your mother by her Christian name. Disrespectful if you ask me."

I'm about to snap back at her and say Mom likes it, but I hold my tongue when I notice how neglected the duplex has become. One thing Annie shares with my mother is a deep love of the architecture and the homes of Bell River. There's no way she would let her own place fall into disrepair if she could afford the upkeep. I always thought Annie was independently wealthy. I guess I was wrong.

Walking up the steps to Mom's door, I spot a birdfeeder hanging from a tree. A red cardinal and his buff-colored mate are pecking at the seeds. Little three-pronged bird tracks cover the snow on the railing. Just like my mom…always feeding something, whether its people, wildlife, or strays. Before I can knock, the door opens. The smell of cocoa and sugar envelops me.

"Jenna Bean!" Mom throws her arms around me. "Guess what I made?"

"Hot chocolate?"

"With marshmallows." She beams.

I follow her into the kitchen, where she pours two steaming mugs of homemade hot chocolate before topping them with two marshmallows each. Outside the window, the birds are chased off by a red squirrel who swings upside down, stuffing his cheeks.

Mom leads me to the living room. On an end table, there's a tiny Christmas tree covered with ornaments I recognize from childhood. There's the plastic roulette wheel Dad brought home from Atlantic City, next to the clay cat with rhinestone eyes I made in school, and the antique wooden drummer boy Mom found at a thrift shop. The tree strains from the weight, and every ornament holds a memory. Wrapped around the entire display is a string of real cranberries.

"I saved one for you to put on." She hands me my favorite childhood ornament, a worn felt polar bear. I struggle to find an empty spot toward the bottom of the crowded tree, so I hang the bear at an angle as if it were standing on its hind legs.

Martha smiles, plops down on the couch, tucks her legs under her cozy sweater, and gestures for me to join her. Sitting next to her now, it's hard to believe she was ever sick. She was a history teacher when our long streak of bad luck hit. First, my dad disappeared. He sent letters for a while, more like elaborate excuses. We got along fine without him for a few years until Mom contracted meningitis and was knocked off her feet for six months. Even with insurance, the bills piled up. Eventually, we had to move to the Scrublands, and Tyler started getting into trouble. I didn't think things could get worse...until they did. During his junior year, Tyler was arrested for murdering our high school football coach, Joe Vitner, and Martha—sweet, bookish, and tirelessly optimistic Martha—lost her teaching job. The school board claimed her dismissal was due to the town's declining population. But they fired her right after Tyler's conviction, making it hard to believe that excuse.

"How's school?" Mom sips her chocolate.

"Tricky. Luckily, I got your brains."

She laughs, and two spotted cats saunter into the room.

"Which one is Eliza, and which one is Alex?" When her beloved tomcat, George Washington, passed away last year, Mom took in a pair of strays and named them after Alexander and Eliza Hamilton.

"Eliza's tail is fluffier, and Alex has that swirly white mark on his back."

I lean down to offer Alex my hand to sniff, but he bolts under the couch.

"He's a bit nervous. He'll get used to you. In the meantime, try this." She scoops up Eliza and gently sets her on my lap. The cat immediately starts purring.

As we chat, I notice a pile of bills on the sideboard, cracks in the wall, and a leaky ceiling. The curse of Bell River has definitely spread to this duplex.

"Oh. This came for you." She pulls a creamy white envelope from the stack of bills and hands it to me.

On the front, my name is written in elaborate cursive, care of my mother's address. I slip my fingernail under the flap, rip the thick paper open, and slide out a gold-embossed invitation.

You are cordially invited to
The Winter Carnival Party
Peyton Honeycutt will host an Informal-Formal Class Reunion
Candidate Woodrow Wade Jr. will be in attendance

"No, thank you." I toss the invitation on the coffee table for Mom to read.

"You can't miss that. All of your old friends will be there."

What friends? Star is the only person I want to see, but now that she's engaged to Woody Wade, I'm not so sure.

"Now, Jenna Bean—"

"I just want to keep a low profile, Mom. Besides, who has an eight-year reunion? That's ridiculous. It's obviously just a ploy to promote Woody Wade."

"Maybe. But it still could be fun. Promise you'll at least think about it?"

There's no use arguing with Martha.

"Want another marshmallow?" I move Eliza to the floor and head for the kitchen.

"I'm good," she calls after me. "I set your room up with all your stuff."

I find the open bag of marshmallows inside a sparsely stocked cupboard. There's spaghetti, sauce, a few cans of soup, and that's it. I check the fridge. It's bare bones, too. I've asked Martha how she's doing a dozen times. Now, I'm starting to get the picture.

"Where's the bathroom?" I call out, stalling for time.

"Left side of the hallway."

I order my usual list from Instacart with a few extras. When I return to the living room, Martha is fiddling with her hands, a dead giveaway she's nervous. I flop down on the couch and meet her eyes.

"So, when were you going to tell me you're broke?"

"The day you have a daughter, you'll understand. It's not an easy thing to say. Besides, I'm getting a check from The Heritage Society in a few days."

"You're working for cranky old Mrs. Dupont? I thought you were tutoring and reselling thrift finds on eBay?"

"Hush! I've also been cleaning houses to make ends meet. Annie's been a real godsend."

The thought of Martha cleaning houses for Annie Dupont makes me cringe. There's nothing wrong with it. It's an honest way to make money, but Mom really loved teaching history. I've never met anyone more passionate about the past than Martha. Things aren't just bad in the town, but also in Martha's life.

An hour later, while we're watching a rerun of *Antiques Roadshow*, the doorbell rings. Martha answers and says, "Are you sure you're at the right house?"

Andy Barnes walks in carrying the groceries.

"You're the Instacart guy?" I say, baffled.

"I'm everything." Andy grins and sets down a bag. "Uber, Instacart, notary, messenger."

"Oh, Jenna Bean," Mom says, "you shouldn't have."

"Mom, I have to have coffee. Sorry, but I'm an addict. I didn't want to tell you."

As Andy brings in the supplies, Mom and I start unloading

coffee, cream, apples and pears, broccoli, cauliflower, bacon, eggs, and bread. The last bag holds stuffing, cranberries, and sweet potatoes.

Finally, Andy drops a fifteen-pound turkey on the counter.

"Looks like the makings of a fine meal." Andy starts folding bags, lingering.

"Would you like to join us for Christmas dinner?" Mom offers.

"I thought you'd never ask." Andy grins.

After a dinner of bacon, eggs, and toast, Mom leads me upstairs to the guest room. I lug my suitcase up the steps. When she opens the door, it's like stepping into a time machine. She kept all of my old furniture and mementos. There's my chest of drawers, desk, and bookshelf filled with dogeared detective novels. My Raymond Chandler map of Los Angeles is hanging on the wall.

"I tried to put everything back the way you had it in your old room. Even your games, see?"

Stacked in the corner is my game collection, including Law Enforcement Edition Monopoly, Risk, Scrabble, and Chess. When we were growing up, Tyler and I used to play while Mom cooked dinner. Martha walks to the bookshelf and pulls out a yearbook. She sinks on the bed and ruffles the pages. It's from Tyler's junior year...he never made it to senior.

"It was sweet of you to get the kids to sign it," Martha says, a numbness in her eyes.

I was already away at college when Tyler was arrested but returned for the trial, and to help with the aftermath. Martha turns to a particular page too easily, as if she's sat here before. There's a picture of the football team lined up, front row kneeling, helmets off. Coach Vitner grins proudly in the back. Tyler's in the center, flanked by the Spar brothers, who tower over him. Ty was a wide receiver. He could run a forty-yard dash in five seconds. Stan and Jay Spar were offensive linemen, always hard to tell apart, freckled and burly, with square torsos, bulldog faces, matching snub noses, and lopsided grins. They were always causing trouble, but being nephews to Stockade Wade and cousins to Woody, they were practicably untouchable.

"Those awful Spar boys," Martha says. "They were a bad influence on Tyler."

"I remember when they TP'd the trees on Main Street."

She smooths a hand over the glossy paper. "I should never have let Tyler near those hellions."

"What happened isn't your fault, Mom."

I squeeze her hand. Martha stares down at Tyler's face. She gets quiet, deathly quiet, then snaps the book shut, shrugging off the darkness eating around the edges of her life.

"Better get some sleep, Jenna Bean. Big day, tomorrow. Thanks to you, I'll be cooking quite a meal."

Martha shuts the door, and I hear her calling Eliza and Alex, who pad up the stairs.

Tyler's yearbook goes back on the shelf as I pull out my own and sit back on the bed. There's a picture of the Raymond Chandler Appreciation Society hamming it up before a portrait of the author looking thoughtful in wire-framed glasses and smoking a pipe. I presided over a grand total of three members: Shane Cross, the emo weird kid who never spoke to anyone but us; Maggie "Magpie" Byrd, the slight, nervous bookworm; and my best friend, Star Simonsen.

I turn the page. Someone I've tried to forget looks back at me—Dylan Connor.

Of all the unlikely long shots, Dylan Connor, the captain of the football team, took an interest in me senior year. It was a short-lived and traumatic romance. My skin prickles at the memory.

It all started at the end of a Bell River High football game. Star was a cheerleader, and I was in the stands, whooping it up every time she did a cartwheel. Dylan came over, flush from the winning game, cheeks ruddy, dark hair tousled, and dark eyes bright with triumph. I thought he was just being nice to Star's friend, but then I saw the look on Peyton Honeycutt's face and realized something was up.

"We should hang out sometime." Dylan smiled.

For a moment, I just stared at him, mouth frozen.

"S-sure," I finally managed.

"Next weekend?"

I forced a nod as my brain exploded with the realization that Dylan Connor, the cutest and most popular guy at Bell River High, just asked me out.

The whole next week, Dylan paid extra attention to me, stopping by my locker and waving across the cafeteria in front of the team. Star even heard a rumor he was thinking about asking me to prom.

On Friday, he passed me a note in Language Arts that read: *Pick you up at dawn tomorrow. Dress warm.* The early morning hour should have been a giveaway. But I just imagined a long drive, a romantic hike, or maybe a picnic.

The next day, Dylan picked me up and drove west into the deep woods. On the way, he told me we were going deer hunting. At first, I thought he was joking. But then he started to explain antler point restrictions (the deer had to have at least one antler with three or four prongs, one inch long), how many deer a hunter was allowed to take, and which were the best trails. Lots of kids at school hunted, but I never had, and I certainly didn't want to. I thought about asking him to take me home, but I was afraid of insulting him and ruining our first date. Besides, I thought. What were the chances of actually spotting a deer?

We parked at the base of a trail. Dylan checked his equipment and showed me the basics of handling a gun. He said his father had taught him years earlier. Then we started into the woods. The day was cool and crisp. Dylan was enthusiastic and confident. He could read tracks and showed me how to stay downwind of the prey and use the terrain to keep hidden. We also talked about school, our families, and future plans. I managed not to think about why we were there and just enjoy his company and the beauty of the woods. Eventually, we took a break and sat on a fallen tree, sharing trail mix. I had never felt so at ease with a guy before.

"I know this is our first date, but I really like you, Jenna," he said.

"Me too." My stomach fluttered.

"So, do you want to go to the prom with me?"

"That would be great." I hoped my smile wasn't so huge that I looked insane.

"It's a date." His deep brown eyes smoldered, and I thought he might kiss me. Instead, he hopped up. "Now, let's go bag a deer."

By noon, we'd spotted a buck with heavy antlers. Dylan was excited. This wasn't just any deer but an older buck, a real prize. We stalked the graceful deer through the rocky trails. I intentionally stepped on twigs and leaves a few times, hoping it would hear me and run off. Each time, Dylan shot me a stern look, reminding me to be quiet. When the buck finally took a downward path, Dylan led me to a position behind a rock, handed me his rifle to hold, and gestured to stay still. Sure enough, the buck stepped out of a glade below us, walking delicately as if in a dream. Dylan pressed the rifle against my shoulder and nodded. Panic squeezed my chest. He expected me to take the shot.

I aimed, deer in my sights, and held my breath. But instead of pulling the trigger, I froze.

"Take the shot," Dylan whispered.

"I can't—"

Dylan looked stunned. He pulled the gun away and tried to line up the shot. But the buck's ears pricked up as he caught our scent. There was a loud crack as the shot rang out—and missed. The deer sprang away, disappearing into the tree line.

"Damn it!" Dylan said. "Did you see those horns? You had him in your sights!"

"I'm sorry, it just seems so wrong. The deer looked so... innocent."

"Innocent? He's game. Everyone hunts around here."

"Not me." I smiled meekly.

"Then you should have said something."

I'll never forget the look on his face—like he'd lost all respect for me.

We hiked back to the car in silence. And after a long, awkward drive home, Dylan dropped me off.

After that, he was distant. I would see him across the lunchroom or in the hall, and he was polite but cold. His teammates started calling me "Scaredy Stack," and the nickname stuck. Through the grapevine, I heard he asked Peyton Honeycutt to the prom. When the time came, I stayed home, too humiliated to show my face. I couldn't wait to graduate and get out of Bell River.

I shake off the memory, close the yearbook, and put it back on the shelf. Like my friend Dave says: You can't go back. You can only move forward.

Chapter 2
Bell River Heritage Society

I pull on a robe, grab my phone, and follow the smell of Christmas to the kitchen. It's obvious Martha's been up for hours. The turkey is roasting in the oven, and a homemade apple pie is cooling on the counter. I peek into the living room and find her curled up on the threadbare couch, with Alex in her lap, gazing wistfully out the window. She seems so peaceful with the light on her face and the purring cat.

"Merry Christmas."

She and the cat pivot their heads toward me in unison.

"Merry Christmas, sweetie." She pats the seat next to her. "I was just thinking...this is our fourth Christmas without Ty."

I join her, and we sit in moody silence for a moment. There's a question gnawing at me that I've wanted to ask. "Why did you stay here, Mom?"

She shakes her head. "It's hard to explain."

Usually, I don't like to push her. But the way she's settled into a quiet resignation bothers me.

"You're still so young. You could make a new life someplace else."

"It's not that simple."

"You aren't waiting for Dad, are you?" My father, Vinny Stack, took off when I was twelve. Years later, I came to realize he was more of a grifter than a charmer. But when they were together, he treated Mom like a princess. She was devastated when he left.

"Goodness no. That was a lifetime ago." She points out the window. "It's the town. Bell River is going through tough times. We all are. But I love it. The history, the beautiful old homes. And there are good people here."

I will never understand the hold Bell River has on my mother, as if the trauma she suffered here—Dad leaving, her illness, Tyler's arrest—tied her to this town like a victim to an abuser. All the bad memories just make me despise this place.

"Breakfast first or a walk in the snow?" she asks brightly. Martha doesn't dwell on uncomfortable topics.

"How about gifts first?" I pull a shiny wrapped package from under the tree. She takes the striped foil present I've been hiding. "Go ahead," I urge her.

A smile spreads over her face as she unwraps the paper revealing *Historic Homes of Upstate New York*, a glossy coffee table book full of facts, photos, and architectural drawings. At fifty dollars, my gift exceeds the Stack family spending limit, but after a lifetime of history stories, I'm glad I splurged.

Martha opens the index and runs her finger down the list of homes. "Oh look...Abercrombie Gardens, Arrowhead Lodge," she reads aloud with reverence.

"I checked. The Bradford Mansion is in there."

"So it is...I love that old place. It's perfect, Jenna. Thank you."

My phone chimes, interrupting the moment. I don't recognize the number, which means it's either a telemarketer or Tyler calling on a burner phone from prison. Seeing as it's Christmas morning, I'm betting on Ty.

"Hello?" I answer, switching the phone to speaker mode.

Tyler's familiar voice fills the room. "Merry Christmas."

Mom leans over the phone. "Honey! Merry Christmas! How are you?"

"I'm fine, Mom."

"Really? That's good to hear."

I listen to the two people I love most in the world struggling to communicate. Tyler tries to sound upbeat, and Martha tries not to sound worried. But they can't ignore the awful fact that Tyler is calling from prison. As the conversation grows awkward, I jump in.

"Guess who's running for Congress, Ty."

"Whacked Out Woody Wade," he snorts. "What a joke."

"How'd you hear?"

"I got a letter from Star. Did you know they're engaged?"

"Old Andy Barnes told me yesterday."

"He's still around?" I can hear the hint of a smile in Tyler's voice.

"Yep, and going strong."

There's a pause, and I hear loud clanging in the background—my heart races.

"Tyler? Ty?"

"Yeah, yeah. I'm here. Listen, can you do something for me?"

"Of course."

"Check on Star. I'm kinda worried about her. We exchanged a few letters back and forth. She seems...sad, or lonely, or something."

"Sure, Ty." I didn't know that Tyler and Star were writing. Star was always so popular with everyone, even the mean girls. I can't imagine her being sad or lonely, ever. Although I also can't imagine her being engaged to Woody Wade. "I'll check in on her. I promise."

"Cool. Listen, I gotta go."

"Okay. Love you. Say bye to Mom."

I hand the phone back to Martha so she can say goodbye and leave the room. This seems like the perfect time to share the news about Tyler's case. I search through one of my bags and grab the manila envelope Cole Braedon gave me. But when I return clutching the information that might set Tyler free, I find Martha sobbing softly.

"Hey, don't cry. I have some good news." I hand her the envelope in exchange for my phone.

"What's this?" Martha sniffs.

"New evidence in Tyler's case. I think it can help prove he's innocent."

Her shoulders slump. "That's the real reason you're here, isn't it? Not for school but to snoop around." Her shoulders tense up.

"I am getting school credit for my internship, but—"

She tosses the envelope on the coffee table without opening it.

"But you chose the Bell River Police Department because of Tyler's case, not to spend time with me. I should have known."

"I chose it for all of those reasons, Mom. Can't you see this is a good thing?"

"For who? For me? For Tyler?" The pitch of her voice escalates. "You didn't tell him, get his hopes up?"

This is not the reaction I was expecting. I push the envelope back in her direction.

"You believe he's innocent, don't you?" Anger and frustration flare in my voice.

"Of course!"

"Then what's the problem?"

"We've been through all of this. The appeals. Getting our hopes up and stirring things up with questions. I have to live here, Jenna. And Tyler has to live...there. It's not fair."

Martha bows her head. There is nothing worse than watching your mom fall apart.

"You're right, Mom, it's not fair that my brother—your son—is in prison for a crime he didn't commit. And it's not fair the murderer is walking free. The whole situation is criminal. But if there's even a possibility of clearing Tyler, I have to try. Do you see that?"

She looks up at me, trembling—a tear slides down her cheek.

"What if it's dangerous? I can't lose you too," she stutters between tears.

I wrap my arms around her and she surrenders to her grief, body sobbing and shaking against mine. I've seen my mother cry many times, but never with such abandon. There's nothing I can say to console her, so I just hold her close until she exhausts her tears.

"I know this is hard for you, for all of us," I whisper. "But you taught me that I have to be strong. We have to do this, Mom."

She sits up and wipes her face with the back of her hand. "I understand, Jenna Bean. I do. You always were the strong one. Just promise you'll be careful."

I nod, and she pats my knee.

"Time for your gift, then. Come on."

I follow her out the front door and through the yard. It's freezing.

"Where are we going?" I say as we trudge through the newly fallen snow.

"You'll see," she says, turning the corner.

There, parked in the alley behind the duplex, is my sagging, rusted old Honda Civic from high school. I assumed it was in a junkyard by now.

"The Green Machine? You saved it?" I can feel the smile freezing on my face. The weird shade of teal was an old Honda color called Tahitian Green Pearl. What can I say, it's vivid. "This is, uh...great."

"I had it serviced and new tires put on." She hands me the keys.

"That must have been expensive." I shake the keychain, which still has a green-haired troll attached.

She shrugs. "I thought you'd like some independence while you're here. Especially if you're planning to investigate."

"Glad you're on board," I hug Martha tightly. "Don't worry. This is sleepy little Bell River. What's the worst that can happen?"

~

"Hurry up Jenna Bean. I don't want to be late." Martha buttons her coat and races along the sidewalk.

The Bell River Historical Society is housed in a beautiful, old Victorian home on Main Street—at least that's how I remember it. But racing up the porch stairs behind my mother, I notice the steps are cracked, and the banister is wobbly.

Inside, the dark wooden floor is polished to a high sheen, but the wallpaper and drapes are faded. There are plenty of homes in worse shape in Bell River, including the place my mother rents from Annie Dupont. But this old beauty is definitely showing some wear.

We hang up our coats in the foyer and are immediately confronted by an imposing grand dame greeting guests at a lectern. Her softly frosted hair, pink Chanel suit, and sparkling jewelry contrast with a sour expression. It's been years since I've seen Mrs. Downing, eldest daughter of one of the richest families in the area. She married and moved to Chicago when Tyler and I were kids. She must be in town for the holidays.

"Martha Stack?" She greets Mom like an unwanted intruder.

"Emma. So nice to see you," Martha replies sweetly. "In town for Christmas?"

"Visiting Daddy in the home. What are you doing here?"

"You remember my daughter?" Mom ignores the question and gestures to me proudly. "Jenna is a detective in New York City."

This is not entirely true. I only solve crimes occasionally, but I can't blame Martha. A detective sounds better than a part-time student, bartender, or pet sitter.

"Emma's family are among our biggest contributors," Mom tells me.

The stately woman scans me up and down. I've tried to look presentable for Mom's sake in a black wool dress, leggings, and boots. But I can tell by Emma's scowl that my efforts do not meet her standards. She turns back to Martha with a plastic smile.

"Surely you aren't still a member here? There are dues. Rules." Emma shifts her weight to block our entrance to the parlor.

Martha fidgets with a button on her jacket. "Well, of course I am."

Emma glances into the dining area, where twenty or so silver-haired ladies are seated around tables waiting for the society's monthly tea to begin. Several members are watching the exchange and whispering to each other. A satisfied smirk crosses Emma's lips. She actually enjoys causing a scene. I'm formulating a scathing comment when, to my surprise, Annie Dupont appears. "Martha! Jenna! Come join me." She whisks us to her table.

Emma Downing frowns and turns back to the lectern.

Once seated, with my napkin in my lap, I look around. The room is only half full and the youngest person is at least twenty years my mother's senior. The upholstery is lightly frayed as are some of their dresses. The china is chipped, and the white table-cloths are yellowing. But the members sit primly and proudly, chatting away happily as if they are awaiting service at a five-star hotel. Mrs. Dupont leans in conspiratorially.

"Don't let Emma bother you, Martha." Annie straightens the large bumble bee pin on her jacket. "She's been in a bad mood since one of her precious sons got caught playing around on his wife. Big public scandal."

My impression of Annie so far is that she's a curmudgeonly snob. But I'm seeing a new side of her today. This is the first time she's been protective of Mom. Maybe I misjudged her.

"I don't want to cause a fuss," Martha says.

"Tsk. You know more about the history of Bell River than anyone," Annie continues. "And I told Emma, you do our book-keeping and help me with the gardening. That makes up for not being able to pay your dues."

Mom smiles meekly, and my temper flares again. Why does she put up with these people?

A sullen teen arrives, pushing a tea trolly laden with surprisingly exquisite-looking finger sandwiches, scones, and cakes.

"English Breakfast or Darjeeling?" He sets up our feast before moving on.

"The food is so much better since I suggested we hire Boomer," Annie says, congratulating herself. Then, she launches into a ten-minute monologue about her importance to the town and historical society, her distant relationship to the regal Dupont family, and her belief that the real estate market will pick up soon.

"That Emma Downing," Annie complains. "Wielding her power and bossing me around. I mean I'm the President, not her."

"And you appreciate history," Martha adds quietly.

I nod, sip, and nibble, wondering how my kind, sunny mother tolerates this negative, self-obsessed woman.

"And what have you two been up to?" Annie says. "I've hardly seen you since Jenna arrived."

This seems like a strange question since it's only been a few days. But at least she's stopped talking about herself.

"Oh, we've been having a wonderful time—"

"Well, that's good. But I have a nice couple from the city coming to look at the Bradford Mansion this weekend. I'm going to need you to clean it."

"Of course, Annie. I'll get that done this afternoon. Have you given any more thought to study hall?"

"Study hall?" This is the first I've heard of this idea.

"Oh, yes." Mom's face lights up. "Annie has so many lovely homes for sale, some fully furnished. And not all of the local families can afford tutoring. I thought if she donated the space, I'll donate my time. Kids who need a little extra help or just a comfortable place to study can come to do their homework, and I'll be there to chaperone and answer questions."

"That's a great idea, Mom."

"It's a terrible idea," Annie sputters, slicing through a scone with her butter knife. "All of those filthy hooligans in my lovely homes."

"They're kids, not hooligans," Martha says soothingly. "I was a teacher. I can control a room full of kids—"

"From bad families," Mrs. Dupont insists. "Those low-rent apartments on the west side of town? I don't trust them."

I almost open my mouth to argue, but Martha surprises me.

"Don't be ridiculous, Annie," Mom scolds. "You trust me, don't you?"

Annie lifts an eyebrow and cocks her head. I have to hide my smile. This is the most backbone I've seen from my mom all week. But Mrs. Dupont leans back in her chair, cheeks flushed with anger, and dabs at the corner of her mouth. Then she delivers a zinger.

"Of course I trust you, Martha...but—"

"What?" Martha says.

"You weren't able to keep control of Tyler, were you? The boy ended up in terrible trouble...in prison."

My mother's face drains of color, and she freezes.

That's it. I am officially over this luncheon. I throw my napkin down and stand up. Then I lean on the table until Mrs. Dupont and I are nose to nose.

"Don't you ever talk to my mother like that again," I say in a low voice, seething. "And don't talk about my brother. Understand?"

Annie Dupont shrinks away from me, but she nods in agreement.

Suddenly, the sounds of spoons striking water glasses fills the air. Emma Downing stands up and smiles in her pink Chanel suit.

"Welcome to the Bell River Heritage Society, where we try to preserve the traditions of our fair town. Let's all rise and recite the town motto..."

But I've had enough. "I need some air. See you at home, Mom."

No one else notices as I grab my coat and walk out into the bright winter sunlight, hands shoved in my pockets. Everything's within walking distance of Main Street. I can see my breath as I hurry down the street. How dare Mrs. Dupont speak to my mother that way! I'm back to my original assessment of Annie Dupont being a crass and tasteless, fair-weather friend, depending on the whims of her ego.

I'm still fuming as I pass Mr. White's drugstore. The window is old-fashioned, with a mortar and pestle featured and a display of toothpaste. The door swings open, and I'm surprised to find myself face-to-face with Star Simonsen. When she recognizes me, her eyes grow wide.

"Jenna? I can't believe it!" She throws her arms around me, and we hug.

Star is just as delicate and beautiful as I remember—high cheekbones, bowed lips, and long blonde hair. But something has changed. She seems fragile and exhausted. Then I notice the makeup covering what looks like a dark bruise on her cheek.

Her hand reflexively covers the mark. She's nervous.

"Are you in town for the reunion?" she asks.

"No. I'm here for a few months. I tried to reach you, but your email bounced back, and your Instagram profile disappeared. Are you alright?"

"It's a long story," Star says.

"I've got time. Wanna get a drink?"

Chapter 3
Boomer's Bistro

Boomer's Bistro is quaint and inviting, with reclaimed wood floors, green velvet banquets, and circular metal tables. The overall feeling is French café meets cozy neighborhood bar. A place like this would be packed on a Sunday afternoon in New York City. But other than a middle-aged couple sharing appetizers and a few locals at the bar, Boomer's is empty.

"Star, nice to see you." A burly man with dark skin and cropped hair, graying at the temples, approaches us. He helps Star out of her coat and hangs it on a wooden peg. Although he has a slight limp, there's something graceful about the way he moves. "Hungry?"

"Starved." Star smiles up at him. "Jamie Myers, this is my friend, Jenna Stack."

"Call me Boomer." We shake, and my fingers are swallowed up by his hand. Then it hits me.

"Boomer Myers, the football player?" I'm stunned. It's not that I'm a big sports fan. But Jamie "Blastin' Boomer" Myers was one of the best wide receivers the New York Giants ever had. He was also one of Tyler's heroes. At the height of Boomer's career, he was hit by a drunk driver while crossing the street. I can't remember his list of injuries. But he never played football again. What on earth is he doing in Bell River?

"Former football player," Boomer corrects me while helping me wrestle off my jacket and scarf. "Now I'm chef and proprietor of this fine establishment."

As we follow Boomer to a table by the front window, I connect the dots.

"Are you, by chance, related to Cece Myers?"

He grins. "Guilty as charged. She's my wife."

"Did she tell you about—"

"The new intern? Sure did. Jenna, right?"

"That's me."

"How's this?" Boomer stops in front of an alcove with a view of Main Street behind gauzy curtains. Our table is adorned with a tiny green jade plant, a warm, glowing beeswax candle, and a discreet menu card on a metal stand. Across the top is the word Apéro, with a selection of elegant aperitifs and drinks. This must be the French version of Happy Hour. I notice black-and-white photos of Paris on the walls.

"Did you take the photos?" I marvel.

"I did. When I studied at Le Cordon Bleu. That's where Cece and I honeymooned." Boomer's smile radiates with the joy of a man doing something he loves. He turns to Star. "How about your favorite crepes? And a new rosé from Provence?"

"That sounds lovely." Star seems to relax in the peaceful atmosphere.

"And you, Miss Stack?" Boomer looks at me expectantly.

"Same here. That sounds amazing."

As Boomer disappears into the kitchen, I pick up the menu. The offerings range from pomme frites to French onion soup to crepes. It all sounds delicious. But what strikes me most is that the prices are about half of what they should be. "I can't believe how fancy this place is…and so, well, cheap."

"Woody says the town gave Boomer a five-year lease at a thousand dollars a year. Part of the revitalization efforts. And to sweeten the deal for Cece."

"We used to have to drive to Albany for anything better than diner food." I look out on the quiet street. "Do people actually come?"

"Boomer's hoping the word gets out and people start driving here from Albany. Meanwhile, he gets enough business from locals at those prices to keep going."

This is the first time I've gotten a good look at Star's engagement ring. The diamond weighing down her finger is too large for her delicate frame, and it must have cost a fortune.

"It's good to see you, Star," I say and mean it.

"You too, Jenna." She looks at me with a ghost of a smile. What happened to the cheerleader with the goofy sense of humor? Something has dimmed her light. But what?

Boomer reappears with a silver tray.

"Strawberry crepes with rose-infused cream, paired with the la Provence rosé," Boomer says with pride. He sets down two glasses of pink wine garnished with lemon peel, followed by two plates of perfectly folded crepes sprinkled with powdered sugar.

The sweet, buttery fragrance piques my hunger. The first bite is so mind-numbingly delicious that I glance up in shock.

"My God," I blurt out.

"Bon appétit." Boomer winks and drifts over to the only other occupied table.

"Wow, I suppose this deserves a toast." I hold up my wine glass. "To Lara. I was sorry to hear she passed away."

"Thank you. She always loved you. To Lara, best grandma

ever," Star says, clinking her glass against mine. As her sleeve rides up, a purple bruise is exposed.

"What happened there?" I say, pointing to her wrist.

She quickly pulls her sleeve down.

"Nothing. I-I just bruise easily."

I don't buy it. Star used to get banged up in cheerleading practice regularly. If she was more prone to bruising than the average person, I would remember.

"Is everything okay, Star?"

"Sure." She takes a sip of wine. "I just really miss Granny. She's the only family I had."

We eat in silence for a few moments. I savor the tangy sweetness of my crepe and the cool citrus spice of the wine. Lost in her thoughts, Star just picks at her food.

"So, you and Woody Wade are getting married?"

"You must think that's really weird," she almost whispers.

I shake my head. "Not weird, just surprising. How did it happen?"

"After I finished college, I came back to save money for grad school. We ran into each other. He was so sweet..." She trails off uncertainly.

"High school was a long time ago. People change," I tease.

She misses the joke entirely. Her fingers move to her engagement ring, twisting the band nervously. "He wanted to be a speechwriter. But then his dad encouraged him to run for Congress. And Mister Connors got involved—"

"Mister Connors? Dylan's dad?"

"Yep, father of your number one worst date of all time." Star giggles for a moment, then covers her mouth as if that's not allowed. "Anyway, Mister Connors has lots of money and political connections. He's funding Woody's campaign."

"So, he thinks Woody can win?"

"He and Stockade are sure."

"So old Stockade Wade is going to be your father-in-law?"

"Don't remind me," Star says.

"But you'll be by Woody's side. That's exciting, right?" I take my last bite of crepe.

"I guess." She shrugs. "There's a lot of pressure and scrutiny, just being a candidate's fiancée. What I wear. What I say."

"I used to have to twist your arm to say anything at book club."

"That's true. Things are crazy now. Reporters follow me shopping in Albany. Can you imagine? "

I smile. "Not really."

This time, she laughs out loud, and I catch a glimpse of the girl I once knew.

"Things will get better after the election, I'm sure." She gazes wistfully out the window. "I'll start school again and have my own career. There's still plenty of time to have kids."

Star takes another sip of wine. There's something about the way she shifts in her seat and twists that garish engagement ring. She's not happy. I'm sure of it.

"Star, I'm sorry we lost touch, but you can talk to me." I take her hand and push back the sleeve, revealing the bruise. "Are you okay, really?"

Her breathing quickens for a beat. Then she pulls her hand away.

"Remember Abby? Wade's sister?"

"Of course."

"He never recovered from her death. As the pressure of the campaign got to him, he started having nightmares—about her drowning—almost every night."

"That's not what I asked."

Star looks away, eyes wide and edged with pain.

"I know, I just—"

"Is Woody hurting you?"

Star bites her lip.

"He's never hit me, Jenna, I swear. He gets frustrated, grabs me, and pushes me. But he's never hit me. We're going to get counseling as soon as the election is over."

"We? Or he? I know you want to fix things, but are you happy?"

Star looks me directly in the eye—for the first time since we sat down.

"Have you ever wished you could just disappear, start over? Sometimes I think about it. With Granny gone, I could just walk away, pretend none of this happened."

"Is there anything I can do, Star?"

A shy smile crosses her lips. "Come to the reunion?"

Not this again. Peyton Honeycutt's informal formal? What does that even mean? Looking over at Star, I can see she's serious, so I dial back my annoyance. "What's the story with that, anyway?"

"Peyton planned the whole thing. Don't make me suffer through it alone."

"Why don't we both skip it?" I finish my drink.

"Please, Jenna. You don't understand. I have to go."

Or what, I wonder. I catch Boomer's attention and gesture for another round. Then, I vow silently to myself that whatever else happens, I'm going to do what I can to help.

"Fine. I'll go. But we're going to need reinforcements."

I pull out my phone to text the only person who would drop everything for me.

Me: *Still want to visit?*

Dave: *Upstate in the dead of winter? How can I resist?*

Me: *There's a reunion. Dancing. Drinking. Frenemies. Should be awful. Be my date?*

Dave: *Well, when you put it that way. I'm there.*

Me: *Bring the dress I wore to the fête?*

Dave: *Done. I want to see the invite. ASAP.*

Chapter 4
Bell River PD

Bell River Police Station is over one hundred years old, a weathered red brick building, two stories high with tall windows. Two patrol cars are parked in front. As I step up to the double-paned French doors, I hesitate. I admit. I'm nervous. It's my first day, and this internship means a lot to me. I fussed over what to wear last night and finally decided on a black suit with a crisp white shirt. And, of course, a padded parka with a hood since it's 30 degrees outside.

I step through a doorway with the words *Police Department* painted on the arch above. A decal stuck to the glass reads *Neighbors Helping Neighbors.*

Inside, the reception area is stark and uninviting. Scuffed plastic chairs and an old wooden coffee table face a high counter. A long bulletin board displays small-town notices: lost dogs and cats, voting rules, a flyer proclaiming *Vote Woody Wade for Congress!* and a town map.

On the other side of the counter is an open bullpen. Two uniformed officers sit behind computers. Beyond them is a giant whiteboard with dry erasers tacked to the side. A to-do list is scrawled on the board: Town Council meeting, new stop sign, coordination with Fire Department regarding roof shoveling. Wow, rural police life looks riveting.

I recognize Detective Cecelia Myers from the Bell River Police Department website instantly—a serious woman with dark brown skin and an elegant face. Her loose curls are pulled back tightly, accentuating strong cheekbones. She wears simple gold earrings and a wedding band but no rock. Detective Myers swivels her chair toward me, her brows arched in a quizzical expression. She's guarded and aware; nothing is getting past those deep-set, serious eyes. Across from her is a skinny white guy with freckles and cropped blond hair. He has a slight overbite and squints at his computer through wire-framed glasses. They both wear standard blue uniforms with utility belts and radios. Detective Myers' uniform is immaculate, practically starched. Even her boots are polished.

"Coat rack's over there." She points at the puddle forming under my boots.

"Oh, God!" I tug my parka off and hang it on the rack. "Sorry, Detective Myers—"

"Call me Cece. That's Pete Brewer over there. And you must be Jenna Stack."

"That's me, reporting for duty."

"Hey there." Pete salutes with a crooked smile and a guileless expression.

Cece leans back in her chair and intertwines her fingers. "According to Wolfson, you have a detective's instinct," she says, calm and collected, sizing me up. "Is that true?"

"I guess you'll be the judge of that." I adjust my parka on the hook. Professor Wolfson is my formidable criminology professor and mentor with a reputation for high standards. No pressure.

Cece smiles and stands. "Good answer. Bell River PD is a force of two. We have four telephone lines and Twitter and Instagram accounts. First thing in the morning, we check messages. If you answer the phone, take down the details. If someone's hurt, call the fire department." Cece points at the filing cabinet. "Open cases are in the top drawer. Restrooms are down the hall. Now, let me show you the rest of the place."

Cece leads me down a hallway. She has an athletic, confident walk.

"I met your husband, Boomer," I say. "His crepes are amazing."

"He mentioned there was a city girl with a fine appetite in town." Cece stops and faces me. "By the way, I went to school with John Denning. Wolfson said you two crossed paths at a crime scene?"

"Yes, ma'am, I got dragged into a mugging...and, uh, a murder."

She eyes me up and down with a no-nonsense expression. "That's an understatement. I looked into you. In addition to being Wolfson's favorite student, a dog walker, and a bartender, you've helped the NYPD crack a couple of tough cases. Pretty impressive."

"Denning doesn't think so; he says I should stay out of trouble."

"Why?" Cece stops in front of a door and smiles. "Is getting into trouble a habit?"

"I just tend to be in the wrong place at the wrong time on occasion."

As quick as that smile appeared, it's gone.

"It crossed my mind that you might have requested this place for your internship to try and prove your brother's innocence." Cece crosses her arms.

Busted. My cheeks blaze red. She knows exactly what I'm up to. I shouldn't be surprised. After all, she is a detective.

"This internship means a lot to me, Ma'am. I don't plan on screwing it up."

"Then we'll get along fine." Cece stops in front of what looks like a janitor's closet and opens the door a crack. There's a windowless room with a folding table in the center.

"This is the interrogation room. We book people at the front desk, and then bring them in here to question them." She leads me further down the hallway to an open door. The plaque reads *Evidence Room*. There's a wooden counter with a window surrounded by security fencing. The gate is open, leading into a large room with shelving. "This is where you'll be working most of the time." Cece raps her knuckles on the counter. "Ready to meet the new intern?"

"In here," calls a sweet, comically high voice. Where have I heard that voice before?

We step inside, and seated on top of an enormous metal desk is a slim girl, legs crossed, surrounded by stacks of paper, books with Post-It notes marking pages, and open boxes. Her blue-streaked hair is tied in two puff-style pigtails with thick bangs brushing her eyelashes. She wears a vintage dress with a Manga cartoon jacket, black tights, and boots. She looks up at me through cat-eye glasses.

"Maggie?" I say, shocked. Maggie "Magpie" Byrd? Card-carrying member of the Raymond Chandler Appreciation Society?

Her eyes grow wide. "Jenna? Is that you?" Maggie hops down and hugs me.

Cece smirks. She must have known. "I'm going to let you two catch up."

The door shuts, and Maggie stares at me like she's seeing a ghost.

"I can't believe it's you. Wanna coffee?"

I nod. "Sure. You work here? Last I heard, you were off to study—"

"Accounting. But doing QuickBooks all day was boring, so I switched to criminology." She beams.

That makes total sense. Numbers. Details. Facts. "Order" was always Maggie's mystical calling. In high school, she was a walking database of Raymond Chandler trivia.

She pulls out a purple glitter thermos and shakes it, then pours frothy coffee into two mugs.

"Remember Chandler?" She says. "I went out to the kitchen to make coffee—yards of coffee. Rich, strong, bitter, boiling hot, ruthless, depraved....'"

"'The life-blood of tired men.' Of course, I remember!" Quoting Chandler makes the two of us collapse into giggles.

She raises her mug in a toast. "Welcome to my kingdom, Jenna." Maggie spreads her arms towards a few listless boxes sitting on the shelves stacked next to piles of crime books.

"Uh, what exactly will we be doing in here?"

"Oh, just you wait. We have a big job coming in. I'll need all the help I can get."

"Sounds like fun." I chug down my coffee.

The door bursts open. Cece is all business. "We've got a one-forty-five-ten."

"Criminal Mischief," Maggie says knowingly.

"Come on, Jenna." Cece motions for me to follow her. "You can ride along with me."

The fresh snow is turning to slush as Cece drives through town. At the corner is a familiar sight. Dangling from the maple trees in front of White's Drugstore are long toilet paper strips fluttering in the wind.

Cece sighs. "Not again."

"Jay and Stan Spar?" I crane my neck to look up in the branches.

"That'd be my bet. What makes you think that?"

"The Spar brothers have been TP-ing Main Street since junior high."

Cece pulls up to the curb. Seeing our car through the window, Mr. White rushes out, wearing a doctor's coat and a knitted scarf, puffing out clouds of warm breath. He wraps the windshield with his knuckles. Behind him, the storefront has been graffitied. Badly, I might add—zero imagination. Just swear words and phallic symbols.

As Cece steps out of the car, he points at the graffiti.

"You see? They've done it again. I open late one day, and what do I find? Dirty pictures on the wall. Toilet paper in the trees. They jimmied the lock in the back and took some aerosol glue."

"Did they take anything else? Money? Drugs?"

"Nah, the drugs are locked up good. But you need to stop those boys, you hear?"

"All right, Mister White, I'll send the city janitor to clean this up."

"Something's got to be done. I pay taxes, ya know." He scowls and hurries inside.

The Spar brothers are in their twenties and still doing this crap? Some things never change. Once, they wrote vulgarities over the principal's car in shaving cream. If they weren't related to the sheriff, they'd be locked up by now.

Cece picks up the radio. "Hey, Pete. The drugstore needs a cleanup. Looks like the Spars went on a bender again."

"Oh, Jeez, I'm on it," Pete says.

"Keep your eyes open, they might still be nearby," Cece warns. She reaches over, pops the glove compartment, and grabs an extra pair of handcuffs. Then she starts cruising. The car bumps across a series of potholes. Unruly tree limbs hang precariously over the cracked sidewalks. Open garbage cans spill trash into the alleyways. This isn't the town I remember.

"Aren't they too old to be doing this?" I muse aloud, scanning the streets. Everything is quiet.

"Stunted development and no consequences," Cece says gruffly.

"Hey, what's that?" I point to footprints leading down a cul-de-sac.

Cece slows down. There are three figures. Two of them are wearing shiny workout jackets, trendy but useless in this weather. The third one is small and thin in a puffy coat with earmuffs.

It's the Spar brothers, all right, passing a paper bag.

"Look at that," Cece says tightly. "Up to no good as usual."

She backs the squad car behind a snowbank. Quietly, we step out of the car and circle until we have a good view. The smaller kid peers inside the bag.

"Wow, dope!" the kid says. "You sure?"

"Hells yes, bro," Jay Spar says, a bag swinging from his arm—no doubt filled with aerosol glue.

"You'll make bank in no time," Stan Spar says. "Next time, we talk money."

Cece looks at me in disbelief and leans closer. "Follow my lead. Be ready to run."

"Jay and Stan Spar?" she says and steps into the open. "I want a word with you."

All three suspects take off, legs churning the snow. Cece signals for me to pursue and dodges left. Luckily, I wore my boots with the heavy treads.

"Hey! Stop!" I yell.

Jay looks over his shoulder and nudges his brother. They run faster. Then, out of nowhere, Cece steps out and slams Jay high on the chest. He falls hard and slides on the slushy cement. Stan stops, confused, and tries to turn around. As he runs past me, I sweep my leg out. Stan flies in the air, landing hard on the cement, banging his head. He tries to get up woozily, but I drop a knee on his chest as Cece twists Jay's arm into compliance. She tosses me a pair of handcuffs with her free hand. Damn, she's good.

Before Stan can struggle up from the ground, I jam his head into the melting snow, wrench his arms behind him, and snap on the cuffs.

"Make sure he can breathe," Cece calls out.

Stan looks at me, face wet with slush. "Jenna Stack? Are you kidding me?"

"No way," Jay says and starts laughing. They hoot like a pair of hyenas.

With his free hand, Jay starts texting, thick fingers move like lightning. Cece knocks the phone out of his hand and finishes cuffing him. The third kid is nowhere to be seen, but he dropped the bag.

"Use these." Cece tosses me a balled-up pair of gloves and starts reading the brothers their Miranda rights.

I leave Stan in the slush and pick up the bag. Inside are a few sheets of blotter paper with smiling cartoon cats printed on each tab. Wet with snow, they're disintegrating before my eyes.

I hold open the bag for her to see. "Looks like K2 or LSD, a Schedule One drug—"

She peers inside. "Not exactly. It's called Happy Kat. Popping up around the Upstate region, infused with a compound N-BOMe, known on the street as N-Bomb."

"I've never heard of it."

"It's a hallucinogen. The chemical structure is modified just enough to make a conviction tricky. If it were LSD, it would be a Schedule One, but this is a designer drug." Cece turns her attention to the Spars. "Not very smart TP-ing the trees, boys. Were you trying to draw my attention? Where'd you get the Happy Kat?"

"That's not ours," Jay says.

"Yeah," Stan adds. "That kid was trying to sell to us."

The Spar brothers snicker. They look rough, with dark circles under their eyes, like they've been up all night. Older and shaggier, but basically, the same chunky thugs I remember.

"I'd be careful if I was you, Officer Myers. Uncle Wade's not going to like you framing us," Jay taunts.

"Yeah," Stan says. "I wanna speak to my lawyer."

That hasn't changed either. They're still disrespectful jerks.

Cece pulls on gloves and conducts a weapon search. Jay is clean. When she turns to Stan, she pulls a Ziploc bag full of Happy Kat out of his inner pocket—the mother lode.

Her eyes grow wide as she radios. "Hey, Pete? You know that Happy Kat sample we've been trying to get? I think I have it. And we've got a couple of special guests arriving for booking."

Chapter 5
The Vault

Officer Pete stomps his feet in the cold outside the station. When the police sedan rolls to a stop, he slaps the side of the patrol car and opens the door. "Welcome, boys," he chirps with a satisfied grin on his face.

The Spar brothers shrug out of the sedan, handcuffed and disgruntled.

"Search them again," Cece says. "They've been way too quiet."

"You wouldn't play your Aunt Cece and Uncle Pete, would you?" Pete pats the Spars down. When Stan refuses to open his hands, Pete pries his fingers back one at a time.

"Right again, boss." Pete holds up a partially dismantled binder clip.

I learned in lock-picking class that a binder clip can be turned into a functional handcuff key. Stan must have been working that clip on the ride back to the station.

Pete tosses the confiscated tool to Cece.

"Still got that ridiculous YouTube channel, Stan?" she says.

"We broke a hundred thousand followers," he answers proudly. "More money than your crap job."

"Did you do us the favor of posting your most recent stunt?"

I check my phone. Sure enough, the Spars have a YouTube channel called "Bro Time." There must be a hundred videos of them doing stupid pranks and dangerous stunts. The last post, uploaded yesterday, shows Stan hydroplaning a car in an icy parking lot.

"Uncle Wade will destroy you, dimwit," Jay Spar warns, face twisted and red.

"Boo hoo," Pete says, grabbing their collars.

They trudge up the steps reluctantly.

A blast of warm air hits us as we step inside the station. Officer Pete shuttles the Spars into the bullpen and sits them in chairs.

"Hey, Cece? What are the charges?" Pete takes a seat behind his computer.

"Destruction of property, resisting arrest, possession of a controlled substance—"

"Bullshit," Stan says. "Happy Kat is legal—"

"Shut up, genius," Jay hisses. "We wanna speak to our lawyer."

"As soon as we book you, that's your right," Cece says. "Thanks to your ongoing petty crime spree, your mug shots and prints are already in the system. Once you call your lawyer, I'm calling the state cops. Because of you two, the drug trade in Bell River is booming, and I'm fed up."

"No idea what you're talking about," Jay snickers. Stan erupts into laughter and kicks Jay's chair.

"Settle down!" Cece snaps. The room grows quiet. "First, it was pot, then oxy, and now Happy Kat. You don't listen, no matter how many times I tell you. The facts are you're hurting people. That ends today." She leans in, voice low. "If I were you boys, I'd start praying."

For the first time, Jay reacts with a whiff of fear. Stan appears to be too dumb to understand this isn't just another vandalism charge. They're in serious trouble.

"You first, Jay." Officer Pete opens the booking program in his computer. "Name?"

"First name 'I want,'" Jay sneers. "Second name, 'my lawyer.'"

"Yeah," Stan echoes, crossing his arms. "Same here."

Pete shakes his head and enters their names in the system. "Let's see, time, eleven a.m., place, Bell River. What street did this incident take place on?"

"Maple Street," Cece says.

The Spars are not cooperating. They shrug, shuffle their feet, and deflect questions as Pete fills out the form.

"Looks like we hit the jackpot." Pete smiles. "Jason and Stanley Spar have new warrants out of Albany. You're going to need that lawyer, boys."

"Don't bet on it," Jay says. "Uncle Wade's got friends everywhere."

"Is there a way to trace the Happy Kat blotter?" I ask. "To the original chemist?"

"Get a load of Stack," Jay says. "You were always a loser. Now you're a wanna-be cop, too?"

"We'll need a warrant to get their phone contacts," Cece says. "Find out who's buying and selling."

Cece strolls over to the desk, pulls on a fresh pair of black latex gloves, and carefully arranges the evidence on the counter: the Spars' phones, the stolen bag of spray glue, the Ziploc filled with Happy Kat, and the recently acquired binder clip.

"Whoa," Pete says, seeing the amount of blotter paper. "A haul that size should get us on the front page of the *Albany Star.*"

"Maybe the FBI will finally take notice." Cece reaches for the evidence bags—the box is empty.

"What the hell, Pete!"

"Sorry, ma'am, I used the last one."

"It's bad enough when you don't replace the toilet paper, but the evidence bags?" She turns to Jenna. "I need you to run to the evidence locker and get some bags. We've got to seal the blotter and phones before..." Cece trails off nervously.

"Before what?"

"Just find Maggie and get those supplies," she barks. "Now."

I rush down the hall to the evidence room, grab the door jam, swing around the corner, and run inside, breathless. Maggie is seated on top of a table, legs crossed, face buried in a massive book titled *Learning Evidence: From the Federal Rules to the Courtroom*. A lamp is swung over the book, and she's trailing a finger down a page. A rainbow of stickies marks various sections. She ignores my clattering entrance.

I take a deep breath before the words tumble out. "Cece sent me to—"

"Shhhh. I'm at the part about how 'writings' include photographs, video, and other media. Do you know what that means? A screen capture of Snapchat would be totally legit."

"I got the feeling it's kind of urgent," I manage while catching my breath.

Her poufy blue ponytails bob as she looks up at me curiously, like the Cheshire Cat in *Alice in Wonderland*. Or is it the caterpillar? Reluctantly, Maggie puts a bright pink stickie note on the open page and closes the book.

"What do you need exactly?" she says, legs dangling over the table.

"Evidence bags."

"Over there." She points to the supply shelf and turns to grab the office stock list.

I start looking through the shelves searching for a box of evidence bags. "Where exactly? I'm not seeing them."

"You'll probably need that stepladder," she says. "Top shelf."

I grab the ladder, pull it open, and slot the side rails in position.

"One times box of evidence bags," Maggie says, checking off the item. "Why does Cece need them anyway? Find something juicy?"

"They're booking Jay and Stan Spar—"

Maggie sits bolt upright. "The Spar Brothers? Why didn't you say so? On what charge? We've been trying to stop those jokers forever. Hurry!" She rushes over and scrambles up the ladder, pushing items aside until she finds the bags. Then she hurries back down and shoves the box into my arms.

"This is what she needs. To preserve the chain of evidence, we have to seal the bags, date them, and write the report before—"

She stops mid-sentence, cheeks red.

"Before what exactly? Why the rush?"

"Trust me, you don't have much time. Get these to Cece now!"

Chapter 6
Stockade Wade

I dump the evidence bags on Cece's desk.

"Give me one of those, quick," she says, motioning me over, tension in her voice. I slap a pile in her hand and she starts the process of bagging and tagging. "We've got two phones, spray glue, a Ziploc filled with suspected illegal substance Happy Kat—"

"How do you spell that?" Pete asks.

"Happy is the way is just how it sounds, and Kat is K-A-T—"

Then, without warning, the bell above the police station door jingles.

Sheriff Woodrow "Stockade" Wade, Sr. steps inside. With his barrel chest, cowboy hat, and "I'm the law" swagger, he's the same walking cliche I remember from Tyler's trial. But he's aged a bit. His hair is graying at the temples, and his hands show veins and dark spots.

Stan smirks. "Hey, Unc. What's happening?"

"Shut up." Wade's voice is rough and gravelly. He leans over Pete's shoulder to examine the police report. "So, you caught them TP-ing the drugstore? Real hardened criminals, these two."

Jay snickers, which earns him a stern glare from the sheriff.

"There's more to it than that—" Cece starts.

"That your evidence?" Wade crosses to the counter crowding her.

"We were just bagging it up," Cece says tightly.

Officer Pete watches the exchange nervously.

"Sure is hot in here." Wade peels his standard-issue blue parka off and, in one swift motion, knocks the two phones, glue, and open baggie of Happy Kat to the floor.

I watch in disbelief as the drug tabs flutter to the ground.

"Oops." Sheriff Wade steps forward and stomps on the pile of Happy Kat with his wet snow boots. "Clumsy me. Look at the mess I made." He pulls out a handkerchief, wipes up the ruined evidence and stuffs it in his pocket. Then he grabs his nephews' phones.

Cece's jaw clenches. Officer Pete's confident expression withers, but neither speaks up.

I try to catch Cece's eyes, but she's locked down. If this is what Sheriff Wade is capable of, how did he handle my brother's case?

"That's not fair!" I blurt in their defense.

Stockade Wade turns and fixes his cold, disdainful eyes on me, like I'm a bug.

"What's this, then?" he growls.

"Jenna, meet Sheriff Wade," Cece says.

"I know you. You're the Stack girl." He leans in and looks me up and down with mild interest, then laughs. "You, of all people, should know life ain't fair. Didn't you move to the city?"

"I'm here for an internship." I stand straight and tall, not willing to be intimidated.

"Hey, Cece. Grab me a Coke, will ya?" The sheriff paces slowly, picking items up and dropping them carelessly.

Cece strips off her latex gloves and walks over to the mini

fridge. She reaches inside and tosses the sheriff a Coke. He opens the tab, takes a drink, and leans against the wall.

"What kinda internship?"

"Here, at the police station. I'm a criminology student at U of M."

"That egghead Wolfson still kicking around?"

"He's my professor," I say.

"Why pay for school?" Wade grins. "Your brother's a criminal. Study him."

Jay snickers. Cece catches my eye and shakes her head, warning me not to take the bait.

My stomach tightens, and my cheeks flush with anger.

"My brother is innocent," I say defiantly.

"Sure he is." Stockade Wade smiles, eyes bright. "That's what they all say."

We stare at each other for a moment. His expression is smug. He's goading me, pushing me to lose my temper and do something stupid so he can lock me up or worse. I can't risk getting kicked out of my internship. So I clench my fists and focus on my breathing. I'm not going to give this jerk the satisfaction.

Wade drinks his soda, waiting for my response. When none comes, he loses interest and turns his attention back to Cece.

"Your case is a nothing burger, Detective. Just a couple of kids pulling a prank. Uncuff 'em."

"But—"

"I said uncuff them."

Cece face is stoic as she nods to Pete. He releases Stan and Jay, who give each other a fist bump and race out the door.

Sheriff Wade crushes his Coke can and throws it in the trash, ignoring the recycling bin. Then he tips his cowboy hat to Cece and strolls out, leaving the wreckage behind.

There's a tense silence as Cece nudges an empty baggie with the toe of her boot.

"Damn it," she says.

"We'll never beat him at this game." Pete shakes his head.

"You're right." Cece walks to the Intercom. "Maggie? Get your ass in here. Now."

The sound of footsteps echoes through the hall. Then Maggie bursts into the room. She looks around, taking in the scene.

"Oh God," she says. "Stockade Wade was here?"

"The sheriff may think he's God around here. He's not," Cece says. "Starting tomorrow, you and Stack are going through evidence boxes full time and with a fine-toothed comb. If you find one goddammed thing out of place, report it to me. Got it?"

"Yes, ma'am, I mean Detective," Maggie says.

"Absolutely," I say.

"The only way out of this mess is with hard evidence," Cece says, knitting her brow. "An airtight case. If you find anything out of place, call me."

Maggie and I glance at each other. Someone else might ask for an explanation of what just happened, but we don't need one. Eastmoor County clearly belongs to Stockade Wade. Evidence will go missing, and innocent people will get framed—until someone takes him down.

Chapter 7
Dangerous Territory

Clutching a Christmas tin full of oatmeal raisin cookies, I stomp up the steps to the Bell River police station. After telling my mother about yesterday's confrontation with Sheriff Wade, her response was to bake cookies and tell me the story of Frederick Douglass and the terrible circumstances he overcame. Mine was to polish off a bottle of wine and call Dave to complain.

I push the station door open, my head still throbbing. "Hey." I shrug out of my coat.

Pete looks up from his desk and nods silently. Yesterday's defeat still hangs in the air.

"Where is everyone?"

"Cece's out. Maggie's waiting for you." He looks up at me knowingly. Finding a botched case is a long shot, and we both know it.

"Are those cookies?" Pete eyes the tin in my hand.

"Compliments of my mom." I put them by the coffee station and head to the evidence room. Maggie's not in her usual spot perched on top of her desk.

"Maggie?" My voice echoes off the high ceiling.

She calls from down the hall. "In the vault."

I follow the sound to a large gray metal door standing ajar past the interrogation and evidence rooms. The color matches the cinder block walls so closely, I hadn't noticed it before now.

Maggie steps out, wearing black coveralls and latex gloves. Her hair pulled up into a blue pouf on top of her head.

"You ready for this?" She offers me a pair of latex gloves.

"Ready. And FYI, my mom baked cookies."

"Oatmeal raisin?"

"Yep. By the coffee station."

"I love those."

I pull on the gloves and follow her into the large concrete room. First, the sharp smell of mildew overwhelms me, followed by the anxious rush of claustrophobia. Row after row of water-damaged boxes fill the windowless space. In the center is a folding table, two chairs, and an old laptop computer.

"The flood?" I flash back to the letter Tyler received last spring stating that the DNA evidence from his case was destroyed in a flood.

"Yep." Maggie gestures to a chair. "And our job is to go through every box, catalog, examine, and reseal its contents—all while looking for anything that could incriminate Sheriff Wade."

"Is this everything?" Could the evidence from Tyler's case be in this room?

"This is just what they could salvage. Anything obviously beyond saving was destroyed. Now it's our turn to evaluate and organize what's left."

Hope deflates, but not entirely. If there's any evidence left from Tyler's case in this room, I'll find it. But after seeing Stockade Wade in action, I know these boxes are probably just another dead end.

"I've been slogging through solo until now," she continues. "I'm glad to have some help."

"At your service." I pull on the gloves and smooth the plastic covering the table.

We quickly set up an efficient system. I pull a box onto the table and read off the case number and Maggie finds the case in the database on the computer. She notes the list and condition of the evidence inside each box. Then we rebag and reseal everything, put it in a new box, and relabel it.

Maggie answers my questions about procedure and policy, but the work is slow and tedious. By midafternoon, the weight of poor choices and human depravity starts to take a toll. And no matter how many cases we go through, there's no trace of any tampering by the Eastmoor County Sheriff's Office. Stockade Wade has left a clean trail.

"You okay?" Maggie says, cataloging a blood-stained dress from a domestic abuse case.

"Sure." I finish rebagging castings of boot prints on a burglary case, seal the box, and push it aside. This whole thing feels more and more like a wild goose chase. I pull another tattered box down and read the blurry case number aloud. "Zero, six, dash, five, six, three, two, seven, nine." My heart races. Could it be? I stare at the faded numbers, afraid to open the box.

"That's strange," Maggie says.

Is it Tyler's case? I try to respond, but I'm paralyzed.

"Zero, six, dash, five, six, three, two, seven, nine is a drug arrest."

A drug arrest? Then the number that's been seared into my brain for four years comes back to me: 06-563281. Damn it! But it's close. Maybe Tyler's case is here.

"That's two digits off from my brother's case," I comment. "His ended in eight one."

Maggie's gloved hands fly across the keyboard.

"Same arrest date."

I cut and remove what's left of the seal, open the box, and peer in. There's a baggie with eight white pills and some disintegrating marijuana rolling papers.

"So what's strange about a drug arrest?"

"The perp was Shane Cross."

"No way. Emo Shane?" Proud member of our Raymond Chandler Appreciation Society, Shane Cross was a nerd, an outsider—and, as far as I knew, clean. "He used to sit in the back and draw pictures of anime robots. I haven't thought about him in years."

"I ran into him at the grocery store. He's still a bit shy, but he told me he opened a shop selling collectibles and comic books."

Now that I can believe. Maggie and Shane were both heavily into comics and graphic novels.

"Where?"

"Just off Main Street. Well, it looks like the case was dismissed with community service." Maggie stares at the report. "But that's weird, right? Arrested the same night as Tyler?"

"Maybe Stockade Wade was on a spree that night."

"One more box and then lunch?" Maggie suggests. "Starting with cookies."

We reseal the evidence, and I hoist the next box onto the table. "Zero, six, dash, five, six, three, two, three, seven."

"No such case. Try again." I call out two more likely case numbers with no luck. Maggie peers over the laptop and squints. "What was Tyler's case number?"

"Zero, six, dash, five, six, three, two, eight, one." I blink my eyes and look again. It's a stretch, but the last two numbers could be 81. I reach to unseal the box—.

"Wait!"

I brace myself for a speech about all the reasons we shouldn't open the box, like a possible conflict of interest. Instead, Maggie pulls out her phone and starts recording.

"This is Margaret Byrd, in the vault at Bell River police department cataloging evidence with intern Jenna Stack. We have an illegible case number and are documenting the contents for reference. I am handing the phone to intern Stack to record."

As I take the phone, my heart races. Maggie cuts the seal. I peer inside and immediately recognize the contents. This is the evidence from Tyler's trial.

She carefully holds up each item:

- One pair of white trainers, size ten, barely worn.
- One black ski mask.
- One blue hooded sweatshirt, size extra-large.
- One gray blood-stained sweatsuit, both pieces size large.

There's an assortment of swabs from stained carpet and furniture and a stack of several brutal crime scene photos showing Coach Vitner dead on his living room floor, surrounded by broken glass. Dressed in the gray sweatsuit, his skull is shattered, and the room is in disarray.

I gesture for Maggie to examine the stocking cap, which she does, thoroughly.

Finally, she bags and boxes everything back up. I stop recording and text myself the file. We sit side by side at the computer as she scrolls through the official notes on Tyler's case.

"They never found the murder weapon?" Maggie says, puzzled.

"No. But they found hairs in that cap. An expert testified they were Tyler's."

"None there now. But I think I saw some mucus or saliva."

"Enough to test?"

"Probably."

I pull the report Cole sent me out of my bag and hand it to her. She examines the paper and frowns. "Where did you get this?"

"A friend—someone on the inside I can trust."

She scans the document.

"According to this, the hairs in the stocking cap tested positive for drugs? But I was interning in Karl Haben's lab at the time. Those hairs came back negative. How is that possible?"

"Someone buried this report."

She looks up at me wide-eyed. "That would mean—"

"Tyler was set up."

Maggie looks at me in horror. "If this is true, Haben's expert testimony is a lie."

"Maybe, or maybe he never saw this report."

"We've got to take this to Lieutenant Myers right away." Maggie hits print. Then she grabs the copies with fire in her eyes.

"We may have just found that hard evidence Cece's been looking for."

Maggie grabs the official report from the printer, along with the evidence Cole sent me. I follow her with the box from Tyler's case. We march down the hall to the bullpen. Officer Pete is out on patrol, and Detective Myers is at her desk, deep in concentration. She has a computer program open and frowns as she checks through some data. Without looking up, she points in the direction of the vault.

"I know you two aren't done in there."

"No ma'am," Maggie says. "We found something... unexpected."

Cece folds her hands and reluctantly looks at us both. I place the box on her desk. She looks unimpressed.

"You know the drill. Examine the evidence, rebag it, and note it in the log. This better be more than a mislabeled box."

"Um." Maggie glances over at me. "It's definitely more complicated than that."

Detective Myers raises an eyebrow.

"All right then." She leans back in her chair. "What've you got?"

Maggie places the two documents, side by side, in front of Cece. I hold my breath as she picks up the official report and scans the pages.

Then Cece glances at the box inventory. "This is your brother's case?"

"Yes ma'am."

She picks up Cole Braedon's evidence.

"I wasn't here then, but I reviewed the file before I approved your application—" Cece becomes strangely quiet as she compares the two documents. I know exactly what she's seeing. Tyler's actual lab results show he was never on steroids. It doesn't prove Tyler's innocence, but it casts doubt on the Eastmoor County forensic lab.

Her intelligent eyes dart between me, Maggie, and the papers.

"Where did you get this report, Stack?"

I can't name Cole Braedon. He gave me the information in confidence. All I can think to say is, "A trusted source."

"Trusted?"

"Wolfson knows him," I add. "He works with the Feds."

Cece frowns and looks back at the report, reading the lab results again.

"This is serious. According to your source, either somebody made a big mistake, or the head of Eastmoor County's forensic lab lied on the stand."

"Exactly."

"You worked for Karl Haben, Maggie. What do you think?"

"He's thorough, meticulous, and by the book. I can't imagine he would make a mistake like that."

"Could someone have tampered with the evidence?" I wonder aloud. "Maybe hacked into the lab's computer system?"

"Anything's possible," Cece says. "But the motive would be the same—to frame Tyler Stack."

"There's something else," Maggie says, fishing through the evidence box. She holds up the plastic bag with the ski mask. "I noticed some residual matter on the inside of the material. But there's no record of the fabric being tested for fluids."

Cece leans in to have a look. "Is it blood?"

"Possibly. Or saliva or maybe mucus. It was a cold night."

"That's disconcerting." Detective Myers bites her lip as she looks at the newly bagged evidence in the box. "But it also means we may have DNA."

Is this it? Is somebody with authority finally going to take my suspicions seriously? I should be patient, but I can't help myself.

"You have to reopen the case," I blurt out.

Detective Myers looks at me with empathy. Then she shakes her head.

My heart sinks.

"I can't do that," Cece says.

"But you can't ignore this?" My tone betrays deep frustration.

"No, Jenna," she says softly. "I'm not going to ignore this. I asked you and Maggie to look for anything out of the ordinary, and you found a powder keg. I'm proud of you both. But you've seen how things work around here. This is dangerous territory."

"Think about it," Maggie pleads with me. "We could all be in real trouble."

"But the DNA—"

"Jenna, leave the box with me. I'll put it back after I review the case," Cece says.

My hands ball into fists. But I know they're right. The image of Stockade Wade destroying the confiscated Happy Kat drugs still burns in my mind.

"We need to be smart," Cece continues. "Until we have solid evidence, this is an unofficial inquiry."

And there it is—the magic word. *We*. We need to be smart until we have more evidence. Anxiety rushes out of my body, replaced by hope and gratitude. I'm not alone in this anymore. I have help.

"Okay," Maggie nods. "What can Jenna and I do to help—unofficially?"

"Forget what you know about this case." Cece taps the report on her desk. "What jumps out at you as unusual?"

I run through the timeline of the crime. I know every detail.

"The murder weapon was never recovered," I offer.

"That bothers me too," Cece agrees.

"But according to the report, the police searched for hours." Maggie crosses her arms. "They combed the street, the sewer—"

"If Sheriff Wade conducted this investigation, anything could've happened," Cece says, frowning. "I'm afraid we have to start from scratch."

I see where she's headed but it's the last place I want to go. "Someone needs to talk to Audrey Vitner, don't they?"

Cece smiles. "That's what I'd do, if it was an official investigation."

"I could call and ask if she'll see us," Maggie offers.

"I can't stop two citizens from paying another citizen a visit," Cece says and turns back to her computer.

Chapter 8
C & C Emporium

The car engine sputters as I pull to the curb. Across the street, Audrey Vitner's house is a Craftsman-style two-story, painted a cheerful yellow. Two barren maple trees stand on either side of the porch. In autumn, the golden leaves must make quite a display. A weathered swing hangs from the front porch awning, covered in snow. The thought of Audrey sitting with her husband, Joseph Vitner, in happier times makes me queasy. I turn off the engine, and the wipers die. The wind is kicking up snow flurries, and almost instantly, my windshield is buried.

"Okay, let's go over the facts," Maggie says, holding her phone up. There's a grainy image of the front page of the *Eastmoor Gazette* from the day after the crime. The headline reads: *Head Coach of Bell River Badgers Murdered!* Below the headline is a picture of the Vitner's living room with a broken display cabinet. "One item was missing from the house: a National Championship High School Bowling Trophy," Maggie reads aloud and zooms in on an offset picture of the trophy. She points to the curve of the cup. "Joseph Vitner's head wound matched this shape. Whoever broke into the house shattered the display cabinet, used the trophy to kill him, and took the murder weapon."

"There's something that doesn't add up," I say, examining the photo. "The killer disposed of his shoes, mask, and hoodie. Why take the trophy?"

"Good question. Let's find out." Maggie pulls on her mittens and steps out of the car.

I've been dreading this moment. Audrey Vitner hates me and my family. As far as she's concerned, the Stacks ruined her life.

"What did Chandler say?" I step onto the sidewalk. "'If you're not tough, it's hard to survive in this world...'"

"'And if you're not kind, then you don't deserve to survive.'" Maggie threads an arm through mine. She steers me toward the steps. "You can do this."

"No problem." I feel sick as we approach the door. There's a brass door knocker. No bell.

Taking a deep breath, I knock. A high-pitched bark pierces the air as footsteps grow louder. Audrey Vitner opens the door and peers out skeptically. She's wearing a blue apron embroidered with ladybugs on the pockets and dusted with flour. A tiny Yorkshire Terrier circles her feet. She's tall and long-limbed, and her pageboy haircut is peppered with gray.

Audrey stands at the door defiantly, and her eyes spark with recognition. She glares at Maggie. "I wouldn't have agreed to see you if I'd known you were bringing her."

"Sorry to bother you, Missus Vitner," Maggie says. "We just have a few questions."

"Well, that makes three of us," Audrey huffs. She's aged a lot, but her cheeks are rosy. She looks...what's the word? Steely. Her eyes are no-nonsense. Her plaid sleeves are rolled up, and her hands are rough, red, and flour-crusted—a memory surfaces. Tyler raved about Mrs. Vitner's banana bread, tart fruit rolls, lemon squares with powdered sugar, and flaky cookies with drops of chocolate or caramel in the center. "Well, what do you want?" she says, wiping her hands on her apron.

Maggie looks from her face to mine, watching the drama play out. It's time for my mea culpa, although I did nothing wrong. This situation is all kinds of fucked up. I need to say something, but what?

"I-I know I'm the last person you want to see, Missus Vitner. And I'm so sorry about everything you've been through...but we wouldn't be here if it wasn't important." I take a deep breath. "You see, there may be some new evidence—"

"About Joe's murder?" She stares at me hard as a gust of cold wind whips across the porch.

"Yes, ma'am," Maggie says, rubbing her arms to keep warm.

"What kind of new evidence?" Audrey says, suspicious.

"We aren't at liberty to say." I meet her eyes, and it's hard to face the pain she's been fighting all these years. "We're just trying to get to the truth."

Audrey Vitner seems to sink a little as she lets out her breath.

"Fine. You'd better come in then."

She leads the way to the living room—where we all sit down uncomfortably as if there's plastic on the furniture.

"Go ahead," she says, crossing her arms defiantly, and I don't blame her. In her position, I'd be prickly, too.

"Could you tell us about the bowling trophy?" Maggie begins.

"You mean the weapon that killed my Joe?" she snaps.

Maggie nods. The room is thick with tension.

"It used to sit there." She points at a shelf in the display case. A light shines on a picture of Joseph Vitner as a teenager holding a heavy trophy surrounded by cheering boys. "Joe never met a sport he didn't like. In high school, he was captain of the football and bowling teams. The Bowling Badgers went all the way his senior year, beating every other high school in the country. That trophy was his prize possession. The whole team signed the base. He wouldn't even let me dust it off. Always had to handle it himself."

"And the cup went missing the night of the murder?" I ask.

"That's right." She answers me but looks at Maggie. "I got home from my book club, and Joseph was just lying there by the coffee table with his head all…broken." Her mouth trembles, and the words stop. There's a haunted look in her eyes.

"I'm sorry, Missus Vitner," Maggie says. "I know this is difficult."

Audrey nods, takes a deep, shuttering breath, and continues.

"There was glass all over the floor. The display case was shattered. When they took his body away, one of your people asked me what was missing. That's when I noticed the trophy was gone."

God, this is so awful. It's like crashing a funeral. But there's no way around asking her the next difficult question.

"Do you have any idea why the killer took the trophy? Was it worth anything?"

Audrey bristles. Then she sits up straight and folds her hands on her lap, ready to do her duty.

"To collectors, yes," Audrey says. "One of the boys on the team, Randy Johnson, became a world-championship bowler. Joe told me that trophy, with his signature, was a valuable collector's item."

Maggie and I glance at each other. That little fact wasn't mentioned in the case files. If the trophy was worth money, maybe the killer tried to sell it or even kept it.

"And nothing else was missing?" I press.

She shakes her head. "Not a thing."

"Thank you." Maggie stands up. "This really helps us."

"Now, hold on there," Audrey says. "Maybe you can't discuss the case with me in detail, but I have a right to know what's going on."

She looks at me as if I owe her something.

The fact is, I can't think of a reason not to tell her.

"We have reason to believe someone else was here that night," I explain quietly. I can hear Professor Wolfson in my head. Don't do the work for the witness. Let the silence speak.

There's a light in Audrey's eyes for the first time—some relief from her existential pain.

"You mean someone other than Tyler? An outsider?"

"Yes, ma'am," Maggie says.

Audrey shakes her head, and this time, she looks at me differently, with curiosity. "Well, I hope you're right. It always tore at my soul that I might've baked cookies for the boy who killed my husband."

As we head for the door, something inside me snaps. Maggie feels it, too, and shoots me a warning look. But it's too late. I turn and stand my ground. "I promise you—I'll find out who did this to your husband. I won't rest until I know the answer."

Audrey crosses her arms and looks me over. Then she nods.

"The day you find that answer and prove to me your brother didn't kill my Joe, you come back here, Jenna Stack," Audrey says. "I'll bake your whole damn family a cake."

The door closes behind us with a thud.

Back in the car, I crank up the heater and try to shake off the exchange.

"Well, that was crazy," Maggie says. "But good. We're like Starsky and Hutch."

"At least we have a clue to follow." I rub my hands to get them warm. "The murderer might have tried to sell that trophy."

Maggie pulls off her wet mittens. "But that would be dumb."

"I hate to be the one to break it to you, but criminals are dumb sometimes. We need to find out what it's worth—see if anyone tried to sell it."

"We could ask Shane. His shop, The Curiosities & Comics Emporium, is just down the road."

"Have you been there?"

"No, but I've been meaning to check it out, and this is right in his wheelhouse," Maggie says.

Once the car is in drive, the engine rattles ominously. "Looks like The Appreciation Society is about to have a reunion."

The Curiosities & Comics Emporium sits off the two-lane thoroughfare of Main Street. As we park the car, Maggie seems distracted, checking her phone, doubling up on her strawberry ChapStick, and tugging at a blue strand of hair grazing her cheek.

The front window of Shane's shop displays an original *Alien* movie monster holding a Marvel comic. As we step inside, the *Star Trek* door chime makes a red alert sound. For a second, I almost get vertigo. Every counter, floor to ceiling, is covered in collectibles. There's a life-size Dalek from *Dr. Who*, Monarch Monster models, posters from sci-fi movies dating back to the 50s, and even a collection of antique electronics and ready-to-view old VHS tapes. The comic bins overflow with back issues, while valuable models and props are locked in glass cases.

I snap a picture of the chaos and text my sometime technical assistant, Nadir, who happens to be a total fanboy.

Me: *Check this place out!*

A few seconds later, a text arrives.

Nadir: *Whoa! Where are you?*
Me: *An old friend's new shop.*

Maggie clasps her hands together in ecstasy. She has no idea where to begin in this utopia. She looks like a manga heroine in her natural habitat.

"Hello?" I call out. "Shane?"

A head of dark curls pops up from behind a stack of comics in the back. Shane Cross stands up slowly. The scraggly goatee is new, but I'd recognize him anywhere—pale, with brown eyes behind horn-rimmed glasses. Still lanky, he's sporting a shiny Sharkskin jacket over a Godzilla T-shirt. He stares at Maggie, frozen.

"Magpie?" he says, surprised. "You came." His hands shoot up to his glasses, and he accidentally knocks over a stack of comics, which slide across the industrial carpet.

"Hey there, Shane." Maggie beelines over and kneels to help pick up the mess.

"I was going to stop by the Sheriff's office—"

"Really?" She flicks through the comics, rearranging them.

"Those go in alphabetical order," Shane says helpfully.

"I figured." Maggie hands him the stack. "I also sorted by issue number, with the newest on top."

"Thanks," he says admiringly, placing the comics in a bin.

Sparks are flying between these two. Now I understand why Maggie was primping in the car. She sorts through another pile like a fan-dancing geisha and hands the perfectly organized stack to Shane. They're so wrapped up in their ritual that they've forgotten me completely.

"Nice to see you too, Shane," I say loudly.

He takes his glasses off and squints in my direction. "Well, um...no way! Is that Jenna?" He looks back at Maggie questioningly.

"Sure is." Maggie smiles. "She's interning with us at the PD."

"Cool. You guys want a soda?" Shane leads us to a reading area in the back with an overstuffed couch and two chairs. Then he disappears in the back and returns with three cans of cherry cream soda.

"This place is amazing, Shane." I pop the tab off a can. "How long have you been open?"

"Just a few months. My dad owns this building, so no overhead." Shane grins. "I don't get much foot traffic, but most of my sales are online. So it's kind of like free storage and a place to pack orders. I ship all over the world." He beams proudly. "What are you two doing here?"

"We're conducting an investigation," Maggie says. "We hoped you could help us."

"For you, Magpie?" Shane says wistfully. "Anything."

"Remember the night Coach Vitner was killed?" I watch for a reaction.

"Are you kidding? I was arrested by Stockade Wade the same night. He said I was on drugs, which was bullshit."

He seems sincere. "Remember how the murder weapon was a bowling trophy?" I say, shifting my weight, trying not to get swallowed by the overstuffed chair.

"That's what the newspaper said."

"Well, it turns out that trophy was a collectible—signed by a famous bowler."

"So I thought of you," Maggie says. "Well, *we* thought of you."

Shane's eyes light up. "Whose signature?"

"The Bowling Badgers won the National Championship High School Bowling Trophy. The whole team signed the base, including Randy Johnson."

Shane pulls a laptop from under the couch and flips it open. His fingers move across the keys like lightning. I've seen this before. My friend Nadir is a computer whiz. After a moment of searching, Shane looks up, an expression of triumph in his eyes.

"Randy Johnson won the Masters Bowling Tournament. So... his High School Nationals Trophy would have significance. It could be worth maybe 10K amongst serious bowling aficionados."

"Not as much as I thought. But still, a lot of money to most people," Maggie says, biting her lip.

"Did you ever see that famous lecture on Criminal Mind Theory?" I remind Maggie. "Criminals may experience an imbalance between the part of the brain that mediates impulses—"

"And the part that manages impulses. Of course, I remember," Maggie says. "Even if he didn't plan to sell it, the perp couldn't resist taking the trophy."

"Wow, Magpie, you *are* a cop," Shane says, ignoring the fact that she was just agreeing with my point.

"Can you tell if it's ever been offered for sale?" I ask Shane.

"Let's see." Shane searches through databases, his fingers flying. "I went back ten years on the main collector markets. Nothing. The only other place to check would be forums, but that'd take some time." Shane looks at Maggie with a shy smile. "I could do it for you, though."

"Gosh, that would be great," Maggie says. "Would you?"

I step away from the chemistry experiment these two are conducting. I don't think they'll notice. Even though Shane is clearly tech-savvy, he seems a bit strait-laced. What I need is somebody who'll check the dark web. So, I text Nadir all the pertinent facts about the missing trophy.

Me: *I'm looking for chatter on this item—anything you can find—by any means possible.*
Nadir: *You got it. See if your buddy has a Colossus: Dr. Forbin Project poster. I'm looking for one in pristine condition.*

When I come back, Shane and Maggie are so deep in conversation that they don't notice me.

Shane is holding up a Blu-Ray disc. "Well, if you like that, you must've seen—?"

"*Akira*? Sure, I love the whole secret military project endangers Neo-Tokyo aspect—"

"And the rampaging bionic psychopath can only be stopped by two kids and a group of bionics."

"So cyberpunk," Maggie says, "the same sensibility as—"

"*Bladerunner*. Dystopian to the max," Shane says. "Hey, I was going to watch a 2019—total sleeper but great—called *Alita: Battle Angel*—"

"Didn't that get like ninety percent on Rotten Tomatoes?"

"Ah—em." I hate to interrupt, but their conversation is nowhere close to winding down.

"Gee." Maggie notices me. "I guess we better get going."

"Drop me your number?" Shane says. "In case I find out anything about the trophy."

"Sure." Maggie's cheeks flush bright pink as they tap their phones together and exchange contact information.

"Cool." Shane grins happily. "I'll text you."

I feel like I'm pulling two magnets away from each other.

Outside, snow is falling again. Really? Big wet clumps. We slosh through the freezing puddles and slide into the now ice-cold car. I crank the heat up and wait for the cool blast of air to turn warm.

"So, what do you think?" I ask, trying to stop my teeth chattering.

"His shop is so awesome," Maggie says happily.

His shop, huh? Call me crazy, but it's something *inside* the shop that interests her.

"I meant about the case. The motive has always been a big

question mark. Maybe our perp knew about Coach's prize trophy. In the middle of the theft, Vitner surprises him. He panics and kills the coach. Then our guy ends up stuck with an unsellable murder weapon."

"Uh huh." Maggie looks out the window, distracted. This might not be the best time to spitball theories. After all, she's just had a transcendent experience. I pull up to her doorstep.

"I think he likes you," I say casually.

"Really?" Maggie says. At that exact moment, her phone chimes.

"It's him!" She holds up the screen.

Shane: *Hey Magpie, so good to see you!*

"What do I do?"

Maggie hasn't changed. Whenever she gets nervous, she gets socially inept. This romance is going to need help.

"Ask him if he's got a *Colossus: Dr. Forbin Project* poster—in pristine condition."

Chapter 9
Push Back

After working in the dark, moldy vault all morning, Maggie and I take a much-needed break. We head for the bullpen, where the air is fresher, and pour ourselves some coffee. Cece looks up from her mound of paperwork and tilts her head toward Pete's empty desk.

"He won't mind," Cece says. "He's out on patrol, avoiding paperwork."

The radio crackles to life.

"We got a disturbance on Elm Street," Officer Pete's tinny voice reports. "Mrs. Proctor's golden retriever is on the loose. Again. I'm in pursuit."

"Affirmative," Cece says. "Bet you wish you were doing your paperwork now."

"You're breaking up, boss."

"Don't forget my sandwich." She shakes her head and goes back to work.

I take a seat at Pete's desk and Maggie plops down in his guest chair. Now that we're working together to investigate Tyler's case, I feel better. Maggie and Cece's support has changed everything.

"So, what are you wearing?" Maggie sips her coffee.

I look down at my slacks and tee shirt, confused.

She shakes her head. "To the reunion tomorrow."

"Oh, that." Now that it's almost here, I feel dread. Star's been obsessed with getting her nails done and planning outfits. I swore I'd be there for her, and I will. But the thought of seeing Peyton Honeycutt and her jock friends again reminds me of a nightmare I once had after mixing vodka and pizza. But Maggie is excited to see Shane again, and I don't want to ruin it for her by being negative. "My friend Dave is bringing me my one and only fancy dress." I pull out my phone and start scrolling through pictures. "I wore it to a charity thing last spring—"

The station door slams open loudly, startling us. A gale of brisk air rushes in, followed by Sheriff Stockade Wade. He struts across the threshold, trailed by a pale man with faded, milky eyes and thick, horn-rimmed glasses. A young, nervous-looking deputy follows.

"Holy smokes!" Maggie whispers. "What's Karl Haben doing here?"

Detective Myers looks up from her computer. "Can I help you, Sheriff?"

"Let's see." Sheriff Wade pulls a docket from his jacket and reads. "We're here to collect all evidence associated with case number zero, six, dash, five, six, three, two, eight, one."

My stomach clenches. That's Tyler's case.

"Why exactly?" Cece leans back in her chair.

"Official forensic business." Haben speaks with a slight accent I can't quite place.

"On what authority?" she says calmly.

Wade laughs. "Last time I checked, I was the elected sheriff of Eastmoor County. That case is flagged for reinvestigation in the event of new evidence." Wade folds his arms across his chest and grins. "Your super sleuth here set off alarm bells yesterday."

Maggie's eyes widen. She mouths, "Oh no," but no sound comes out.

"What's he talking about?" I whisper.

"When we—I mean, I updated the database—it must have triggered a notification."

"You can't just walk in here and take evidence," Cece argues.

"Actually, Detective," Karl Haben interrupts. "I can."

"Doctor Haben." Cece turns to him. "I appreciate your position as Chief Forensic Chemist of Eastmoor County, but this is highly irregular."

"Detective Myers, I'm sure you can also appreciate the urgency." Haben plucks a piece of lint off his lapel. His nails are a sickly yellow color. "I am eager to personally supervise and investigate any new evidence in a case where my lab was involved."

I can't tell if Haben's tone is intentionally condescending or businesslike. Regardless, Cece isn't fazed. She studies him indifferently.

"I assume you have the appropriate paperwork?" She holds out her hand.

"The subpoena duces tecum? Why of course." Haben snaps his fingers.

The nervous deputy steps forward and hands Cece an envelope. She slowly tears open the paper and removes the court order, then reviews its contents.

I'm frozen in place and Maggie holds her breath in anticipation. Sheriff Wade strolls over to the mini fridge and helps himself to a soda. After a full minute, Cece looks up.

"Maggie, please show the deputy and Doctor Haben to the vault."

She looks at me in horror and stands up. As they follow her down the hall, something inside me snaps.

"No!" I blurt out, jumping to my feet. "You can't let them—"

"Stand down, Jenna. Everything's in order." She signs the paper and hands it back to Wade. Then she flashes me a warning look—one that makes me freeze.

Sheriff Wade shoves the paper into his pocket. He crosses the room and stops just inches in front of me. I stand up straight, but his enormous presence looms over me.

"I'd think you'd be happy, Miss Stack," Wade says. "Maybe Haben will uncover something new, get your murdering brother sprung on a technicality."

"Tyler didn't kill anybody."

Wade leans in so close I can feel his hot breath on my face.

"Or maybe," he hisses, "Doc will find more evidence that your punk ass little bitch of a brother is exactly where he belongs."

My breath catches in my throat, and the room starts spinning. I can feel the evil radiating from this man. At this moment, I'm certain he knows Tyler is innocent and will do everything he can to ensure nobody ever learns the truth.

Haben and the deputy return, carrying the evidence box marked with Tyler's case number. It's like I'm trapped in a bad dream, running down an endless hallway or being smothered and gasping for air, praying to wake up.

"Always nice to see you, Detective," Wade says, tipping his hat to Cece.

I watch helplessly as he disappears through the door, followed by Haben and the deputy, carrying the box so critical to Tyler's case.

"Jenna. Are you okay?" Maggie's concerned face floats in front of me.

"W-we c-can't just..." I stutter. "Let t-themmm—"

"She just needs air. Come on." Cece takes my arm and leads me out the door.

Outside, in the snowy parking lot, Wade's cruiser pulls away, kicking up ice and gravel. Another wave of panic hits as I watch the evidence that could clear my brother disappear into the distance. The wind stings my cheeks. I'm not wearing a jacket and I don't care. I feel numb. My stomach is queasy; any second now, I'm going to faint or throw up.

"How...how could you let him?" My words tumble over each other.

"Please, Jenna. Try to calm down." Cece leans in close. "Don't let that bastard do this to you."

"But he knows something. I can feel it."

"Take deep breaths." Cece rubs my back. "In and out."

I struggle to regain my composure. Slowly, my breath quiets down.

"I- I thought you believed me." The words slip out.

"Listen up." Cece holds my shoulders and looks me in the eye. There's an odd, incongruous smile on her lips. "I do believe you. In fact, I was afraid something like this might happen, so I switched the evidence boxes last night. Wait here."

Cece walks back into the police station and emerges with my coat in her hand. "Come on. We need to talk." She looks at me with her version of concern, somewhere between glowering and coaxing a crazy person.

Maggie waves faintly as Cece closes the station door.

"No, I'm fine, really," I say and pull on my coat. I'm lying, of course. My lungs are frozen, and now I'm going numb. I'm also mortified that I lost my shit in front of her.

"For the time being, I'm your boss, and I insist." Cece guides me along the street towards Boomer's Bistro. The city maintenance workers have salted the icy walkways, and the crystals crunch underfoot. I try not to think about Stockade Wade's smug face, or me punching his lights out.

Boomer unlocks the door with a grin even though the sign in the window reads *Closed*.

"Hey, beautiful." He wraps his arms around his wife.

Cece holds onto him tightly like she's drawing energy from his embrace.

Gently, he lifts her chin with his finger, so their eyes meet. "Tough morning?"

She nods, and he kisses her forehead. Then he helps her out of her jacket and hangs it on a wooden peg. I pull my coat off and hang it next to hers.

I'm used to seeing Cece as a tough cop, not a loving wife. I'm struck by how small she looks next to Boomer and how gentle they are with each other. Boomer's apron is covered with flour, and the comforting scent of freshly baked bread fills the air, but I still feel queasy. A teenaged busboy moves between tables, placing polished glasses at each setting and lighting the candles.

"Hungry?" Boomer says.

"Starving, and we need a quiet place to talk." She puts her arm around her husband.

"There's a nice spot over there." He gestures to a table near a potted fern. "You've got thirty minutes 'til we open. Croque Monsieur sound good?"

"Perfect. And coffee. We've had some drama." Cece smiles at him warmly. "I'll catch you up tonight."

"I know what that means." He kisses her cheek, then looks my way. "Jenna?"

"Nothing for me." I clutch my stomach. "I'm not feeling great."

"I'll bring you some mint tea. That should settle your stomach." Boomer disappears in the back, and Cece guides me to the table, set back from the windows and tucked out of sight of the rest of the restaurant. The busboy brings us our hot drinks and pours water.

"Did you know Stockade Wade would come?" I brush a damp strand of hair from my face.

"I suspected he might," Cee says matter-of-factly. "Now, drink your tea."

I sip the tea, even though I have a million questions. Weirdly, I start to feel better.

"Then why didn't you tell me you switched the boxes?"

"Because I needed your reactions to be authentic. Look, Wade's no fool. When you showed up in this town, he knew you'd look into what happened to your brother. We need him to believe he stopped your investigation dead in its tracks. Your reaction just bought us some time."

"But you risked your job—you're willing to do that?"

"For justice, sure." Cece laces her fingers and looks at me steadily. "Listen to me, Jenna. If Wade gets that evidence, your brother has no chance. And we sure as hell can't trust Haben. We need an independent lab to test that mask."

Boomer appears and sets down two plates laden with gooey Croque Monsieur sandwiches and piled high with fresh greens. The smell of ham, cheese, and butter wafts through the air, and my stomach rumbles. The mint tea worked. I'm famished.

"Just in case, I brought you one too." He winks at me. "I'll wrap it up for later if you want."

"Thanks, hon." Cece beams up at her husband.

He squeezes her shoulder and leaves us to our conversation.

I take a bite of the salad. The tangy, delicious vinaigrette wakes up my tastebuds. I move on to the sandwich, a perfect balance of salty meat, rich cheese, and toasty bread. For a moment, I'm lost in the joy and comfort of the meal.

Then it hits me. "What the hell was in that box?"

"Nothing very interesting." Cece finishes swallowing a bite. "Old duplicate files, a drugstore ski mask with some aloe vera smeared on it, an old tracksuit Boomer outgrew. I left the original crime scene photos because they're logged in the database which I backed up on a thumb drive. The box just happens to have your brother's case number written on it. If they don't look too closely, they'll think they've got the real items."

I'm impressed. No wonder Wolfson called Cece meticulous. But I know that it's only a matter of time before someone opens that box—tomorrow, next week, or months from now—and realizes the evidence is fake. When they do, Cece will lose her job.

"I'm so sorry I dragged you into this," is all I can think to say.

She shrugs. "I'm not."

"I thought you loved being a detective?"

"I do. And I love this town." There's a loud bang in the kitchen, and Cece smiles. "Not as much as Boomer does. He even loves your silly Winter Carnival. But Sheriff Wade has made my job here impossible. He's interfered with my cases to protect his drug-dealing nephews. My days at Bell River PD are numbered anyway. If I can help right one wrong and cause Sheriff Wade some trouble, it'll be good trouble and a fine way to go out."

Anger rises in me. Cece's a good, honest cop. She and Boomer are assets to this community. What does Stockade Wade contribute? Corruption and protecting the status quo. Cece's right. If solving this case takes him down, that would be a satisfying bonus. I toss my napkin on the table and lean in closer.

"The enemy of my enemy is my friend," I say. "So what's next?"

"Things could get dangerous. Are you prepared for that?"

"I'd risk anything to prove Tyler's innocence."

"You'll need to be discreet, make Wade think you're defeated."

"I can do discreet."

She raises her eyebrows in disbelief but continues.

"You know what Wolfson says. Working a case is like unraveling a knot. At first, the threads are tight, but you just keep working it until they loosen."

"We must be onto something if we caught Wade's attention."

"That's right. I reviewed the case again last night. The clothes and shoes the police recovered? Nobody ever followed up on them. They were brand new. You already interviewed the closest thing to a witness we have...time to trace the physical evidence."

"Then that's where I'll start."

There's a spark of excitement in Cece's eyes as she pops the last bite of sandwich in her mouth.

"Damn, my husband can cook." She picks up her mug for a toast. "To the hunt."

Chapter 10
The Winter Festival

Martha and I lean on her rickety patio railing, sipping tea and waiting for Dave. The sky is clear after light snow flurries last night. Below us, Annie, who is bundled up in a coat, scarf, and crochet hat featuring a large sunflower, sprinkles the shared pathway with salt.

"It's sweet of Dave to come all this way," Mom says, brushing imaginary lint from her sweater.

I smile and nod. Mom has only met Dave once. She has no idea how far he'll travel for the possibility of drama wrapped up in an evening out. The problem is I'm having serious second thoughts about attending the reunion, and I'm not sure how I'm going to break the news to Dave.

We hear Andy Barnes' Toyota 4Runner before we see it. The sleet-covered SUV careens down the street and screeches to a halt in front of the house. The passenger-side door opens, and Dave stumbles out, bundled in his Armani puffer jacket as if on a trek to the North Pole. Andy retrieves a suitcase and garment bag from the back of his car and deposits the luggage in the driveway.

"Got another pickup." He waves and speeds off.

"And just who are you?" Annie barks and wags her finger.

"I'm Dave," he says, turning on his thousand-watt smile. "By the way, super cute hat. Don't you just love sunflowers?"

There's a pause as if Annie is unsure how to react. Dave stares at her, waiting for an answer.

"Well, um, yes. I do. I grow them."

"Ooh. That's wonderful. I have a brown thumb. But my boyfriend is really into plants. What's your name?" He extends his hand to shake.

"I'm Annie DuPont. This is my home," she answers, keeping her hands on her hips.

I should probably call down and save them both, but I'm enjoying the awkward exchange too much. Undaunted, Dave brushes back his perfectly tousled locks and doubles up on the smile.

"Great name, Annie. Doesn't that mean graceful?" He looks around. "Cute house. I love the early American vibe. So rustic— JENNA!" He notices Mom and me for the first time and waves. "And Martha! Don't you look gorg!"

Martha giggles. Giggles! This is the effect Dave has on people.

"Hi, Dave!" I wave back. "Mrs. DuPont, this is my friend Dave from the city. He's visiting for the night. Dave, this is Mom's landlady...and, um, friend." I'm not sure their relationship fits my definition of friendship, but it seems like the right thing to say.

"Any friend of Martha's is a friend of mine." Dave throws his arms around Annie and kisses her on both cheeks, French style. She stands frozen in shock, touching her cheek as Dave gathers his bags and brushes past her to greet us properly.

As soon as we're settled inside, Martha looks at her watch.

"Oh dear, I'm tutoring Andy Johnson at the library at the half hour." She pulls her coat on, and with a whoosh, disappears out the door, leaving Dave and me alone in the house.

"Our humble guest room is this way." I lead him up the steps.

Martha's cats peek through the banister railing at the intruder before darting up the steps and disappearing into Mom's room.

"They're harder to charm than Annie," Dave says, stopping at the top of the landing. "Is that your room?" Before I can answer, he drags his luggage to the doorway and steps inside. He looks around the room Martha set up for me—my game collection, the bookshelf filled with detective novels, the framed photos—and shakes his head.

"Wow. This is like a shrine to your childhood. And you never lived here?"

"Nope." I take a seat at the old, scratched desk where I used to do my homework. "She set this room up just like I left mine at our old place. She said she wanted me to feel comfortable when I visit." A wave of guilt hits me. I rarely visit Bell River—it's too depressing—but I never thought about how my absence affected Mom.

"Well, I think it's sweet," Dave says, walking around the room and brushing his fingers across the mementos. He picks up my senior yearbook from atop the bookshelf. "Been reminiscing?"

I grimace. "Martha and I took a stroll down bad memory lane."

He plops down on the bed and starts leafing through the pages.

"Hayrides? Winter Carnival and Beekeeping club? Seriously J, I can't picture you living here. It's just so...quaint."

There's my opening. I know I promised Star I'd go to the reunion, but now that it's almost here, I feel nauseous.

"Listen, Dave. I appreciate you coming all this way. But this informal formal is bound to be dull. How about we skip the festivities and just hang out here?"

"Don't be ridiculous—ooh!" His eyes light up. He stops flipping pages and turns the open yearbook toward me. "Is this him? The dreaded Dylan Connor?"

Dave points to a picture of Dylan sailing through the air, catching a football. Not even a clunky high school football helmet can hide his handsome face and easy smile.

"That's him."

"Jeez, Jenna. He's gorgeous. You couldn't just shoot one little deer to win his hunky teenage heart?"

I glare at Dave. I know he's joking, but thinking about the awkward position Dylan put me in and the humiliation that followed makes me feel angry and embarrassed all over again.

"Will he be attending the soiree this evening?"

"I don't know. I heard he lives in Albany now, but he manages some family property in the area. So maybe."

"Oh, good. I want him to see how hot and fabulous you turned out. And maybe give him a piece of my mind." He smiles and goes back to perusing the yearbook. I'm starting to worry that inviting Dave was a major mistake when he stops again. "And this must be Peyton Honeycutt? The vixen he took to prom instead of you." He points to Peyton in her cheerleading outfit, kicking a leg up. She's all teeth and long tan legs.

A wave of dread washes over me. Dylan Connor. Peyton Honeycutt. As nice as reconnecting with Maggie, Star, and Shane has been, there are also plenty of people I'd like to avoid.

"Seriously," I plead, or am I wheedling? "Let's skip the party and say we did. There's an amazing bistro in town. I'll take you. My treat."

Dave looks at me with his soulful blue eyes.

"No way, missy. You promised me a party. You're going to deliver a party."

"Really, Dave, I don't think I can go."

He sets the yearbook down and reaches for my hands.

"Jenna, I know this sad little town—and it is a sad little town—has left some scars on you. But you need to take your power back."

"I'm not here to take my power back. I'm here to clear Tyler."

Dave throws up his hands. "Clearing your falsely accused little brother of murder? That's the ultimate in taking your power back. And while you're at it, there's no reason I—I mean we—can't have a little fun. Who knows. Maybe we'll uncover some new clues at this shindig." He points to the garment bag draped over his suitcase. "Now, hand me that."

I pass him the bag. "I know you schlepped a dress all the way up here, but—"

"I did better than that. This isn't just any dress, Cinderella."

He unzips the bag and hangs a dashing gray suit with a white shirt and pink tie on the back of the bedroom door. Then he pulls out a shimmering pink cocktail dress with a deep V-neckline and fitted waist. It's stunning.

"Where did you get that?" I reach out to feel the luxurious fabric. It's light as a feather.

"A client was cleaning out her closet. It's just your size and perfect for you. Rose crystal sequins over tulle. Subtle and elegant.

"It's so beautiful—I can't accept this."

"Of course you can! It was headed for a consignment shop or, worse, the back of a crazy rich person's closet." He shakes the hanger, and the material gleams like a pink fountain. "The magic dress is yours, but only if you agree to wear it tonight."

"Well..." I let the fabric run through my fingers. The dress is gorgeous, and Dave is right. With so many locals relaxed and drinking, who knows what we might uncover?

"Listen, Jenna." Dave counts each point he makes on his fingers. "I'm going to make you go to this reunion thing whether you like it or not. Take the dress. Wear the dress. Be the most fabulous lady there, with, I might add, the most fabulous date."

I bite my lip. He does have a point.

"Okay. If you insist." I take the shimmering confection, hold it up against my body, and look in the mirror. The color is perfect. It brings out the coppery undertones in my hair and somehow gives my pale skin a dusky warmth.

He claps his hands. "Now promise me one thing—"

"What?" I look at him suspiciously.

"Do not Google the dress or the designer. You won't be able to enjoy wearing it tonight if you see the price tag."

I just smile. We both know that's a promise I won't keep.

"Okay, I'll wait until tomorrow," I sigh.

"And no matter what, we're going to do our best to have a fun and fabulous night."

A jolt of excitement runs through me. Dave does have a talent for turning things around.

"I promise."

The sign above the Bell River High School gymnasium reads *Welcome Badgers* and features a picture of the school's mascot wearing a knit cap and scarf. Inside, the Winter Carnival theme is in full swing, with glittery snowflakes hanging from the rafters, enormous fake snowmen, and silver balloons. On the stage, a band featuring Andy Barnes on bass guitar plays a disco tune. People of all ages, dressed in their best party clothes, shake and shimmy on the dancefloor.

Dave and I stop at the check-in table to pick up our nametags and head toward a banner in the far corner with *Informal Formal Reunion—Here* handwritten in badger blue with an arrow pointing.

Halfway across the room, I spot her. Peyton Honeycutt is

standing with Woody Wade and Star Simonsen. She flips her platinum blonde hair, laughs, and slaps Woody's hand playfully. Woody looks charmed, soaking up the attention, while Star nurses a drink and stares off into the distance. I pause under the spinning lights. Is this melodrama how I want to spend my Friday night?

"Come on, hon." Dave grabs my arm and pulls me. "You got this."

He's right. I've got a terrific dress and my best friend by my side. I paste on a smile and match Dave's stride. How bad can the evening be?

As we approach, I see Peyton has done a pretty good job creating a chic little area for our group. There are several high round tables, some comfortable-looking seating, and a long bar with a variety of drink options, including a bright blue punch at one end and imported beers on ice at the other. It's a solid effort at creating a VIP lounge vibe in the corner of a high school gym.

Star spots us and races over. She looks lovely but out of place in a simple taupe suit and low heels, an outfit that screams "politician's wife." I wonder if Woody chose it for her.

"You must be Dave." Star thrusts her hand out to shake. "I'm Star."

"You certainly are, you radiant, twinkly thing."

Her face lights up as he hugs her. Good old reliable Dave. I told him about Star's situation and asked him to be extra nice. He could teach at a finishing school.

Maggie and Shane join us next. She looks adorable in a maroon tulle dress and matching Dr. Martens boots. He's rocking plaid pants, suspenders, a bow tie, and an enormous smile. An unspoken language is emerging between them, shy glances and secret jokes.

We're just getting through introductions when Peyton and Woody saunter over.

"Creepy book club reunion at the bar?" Peyton says with an insinuating drawl. She probably still doesn't know who Raymond Chandler is, let alone ever read an actual book.

"Is that you, Slack?" Woody checks out my dress in all the wrong places before emptying the contents of a flask into the blue punch. "Star said you were in town."

Not that stupid old nickname. How annoying. I smile harder.

"Peyton. Woody. This is my best friend, Dave."

Peyton looks Dave up and down, then at Star. "Quite an upgrade from your high school best friend, I see."

Woody laughs. "Good one, Pey."

Star looks down, embarrassed, until Dave takes her hand.

"Come on, gorgeous, let's dance." He shoots a vicious glare at Peyton and whisks Star off to the dancefloor. Shane and Maggie follow, leaving me alone with my two least favorite people in Bell River.

I take a hard look at my nemesis. Peyton's dress is too tight and slightly ostentatious with odd folds and tassels. Her pout is swollen, and her eyelashes are artificial, like a doll. She looks like she belongs on The Real Housewives.

"I see you haven't changed, Peyton. Still a mean girl."

"It's not my fault she can't take a joke."

I'm formulating a bitchy comeback when I catch a glance of Dylan Connor coming our way. His dark hair is shorter, his face leaner, and he's traded baggy athletic wear for an elegant, well-fitted charcoal suit. But there's no mistaking him. And here I am, standing alone with Peyton and Woody while Dave and the gang shake their booties on the dancefloor.

My fight-or-flight response kicks in. It's been eight years since I've seen Dylan Connor, and I'm torn between two equally unfriendly reactions—slap him in the face or run away. Dave's words ring in my ears: "You got this." I force my emotions into neutral and brace myself for the awkward moment.

"Bro!" Woody fist bumps Dylan.

"Looking good, Dylan." Peyton twists a lock of her hair and leans in for a kiss.

"You too Pey—" He notices me and, surprised, leaves Peyton hanging. The shocked look on her face is worth whatever comes next. "Jenna Stack? I wasn't expecting to see you here. You look... fantastic."

"Um, thanks. Nice to see you." I turn toward the dancefloor, looking for my friends.

"Wait." He places a hand on my shoulder gently. "Can we talk for a minute?"

"Well, the thing is—" I look back at him, searching for an excuse.

"Please?" There's a sadness in his eyes.

"Um, sure." I can't imagine what he has to say to me. But I'm curious enough to agree.

"Drink?" He offers me a glass of the punch.

"Okay. But not that."

At the other end of the bar, Dylan picks up a chilled bottle of white wine and shows me the label. "Will this do?"

I don't know if it's a good wine or not. But it says Chardonnay, and as far as I know, Woody's been nowhere near it. I nod, and Dylan pours two glasses.

"I'm really glad you're here," he says.

He is? That's unexpected.

"You are?" I could say a lot of things, but I keep it simple.

"I've always wanted to tell you how sorry I am about what happened...in high school."

So that's what this is? A bullshit apology eight years too late. I wonder if Star put him up to this crap. I wave my hand dismissively. "That was a long time ago."

"I know, and maybe it wasn't a big deal to you, but it's haunted me."

Not a big deal. Who is he kidding? It was the single most humiliating episode of my high school experience. He was haunted? That's rich. I decide not to let him off the hook so easily.

"Actually, Dylan, it was a big deal."

He grimaces as if I've punched him in the gut but maintains eye contact.

"I was a dumb kid. I thought taking you hunting would show you how cool and manly I was. I never should have put you in that position."

I'm not convinced, so I sip my wine, hoping that if I don't respond right away, he'll keep talking. It's a tactic I learned in school, and it works.

"And the way I reacted, Jenna. I'm truly sorry. I was so embarrassed when I realized my mistake. Ignoring what I'd done was easier than facing you."

"And then Peyton swooped in, and the rest is high school history?" I turn my glass and steal a glance at him. To my surprise, he seems torn up about the whole thing.

"Peyton was just being Peyton." He shakes his head sadly. "The whole thing was one hundred percent my fault from start to finish. Can you forgive me?"

Suddenly, I'm not so sure of myself. He does seem sincere. Why else would he put himself through this high school drama? I feel the weight of the bad memories lighten. If this is what closure feels like, sign me up. For the first time tonight, I feel free.

"Yes. I can. I do."

He smiles, revealing a single dimple on his right cheek that I'd long forgotten about.

"Thank you." We both sip our wine, sharing the moment. Then he tops off my glass. "How long are you in town?"

"Actually, I'm here for three months, interning at the police department."

"Really?" He seems surprised. "What do you do there?"

"File evidence and check supplies." I laugh. "Riveting stuff."

"Isn't that a little...weird?" He gives me his full attention. "You know, because of...?"

"My brother?" I save him the trouble. "Not really. Most of the cases at Bell River PD are small town stuff." I resist the urge to share the developments in Tyler's case. Talking about murder investigations is not everyone's idea of polite conversation. "How about you?"

"I'm in and out of town a lot. Maybe we can see each other again? I'd love to catch up more, when it isn't so crowded."

Butterflies tickle my stomach. Did Dylan Connor just ask me out?

"As long as we don't go hunting," I tease.

His smile drops, and he sets his glass down. Uh oh.

"You know what, Jenna? I never even liked hunting. I just did it to make my dad happy." There's that sadness again.

"Yo, D!" Three jocks in letterman jackets are huddled around the blue punch. "You gotta try this, man. It's sick."

He smiles at them, then touches my arm. "So, I can call you?"

I nod, and he joins his friends. He forgot to ask for my number, but I'm not going to chase him after it. If he's serious, he can get it from Star.

I intercept Dave, who is leaving the dance floor alone.

"Where's your partner?"

He points to Woody and Star, arms wrapped around each other, swaying to a slow tune.

"He cut in, all apologies, and *I love you, babe.*"

"And she ate it up?"

"Yup. Happy as a clam. Unlike the girlfriend."

He gestures to Peyton. She's standing with a group of people, but her eyes are burning into Woody as he twirls Star on the dancefloor.

"You think?" I never thought about it, but now that I see them together…

"Oh, honey. Put on your detective hat. Those two are sleeping together."

The thought repulses me. Then again, they're kind of perfect for each other.

Maggie and Shane float by us, deep in discussion. As they pass by, we catch snippets of conversation.

"There's blue meth in *The Walking Dead* and *Breaking Bad*," Shane says.

"Are you saying that—" Maggie says.

"*Breaking Bad* is the prequel to *The Walking Dead*," Shane says.

"That's genius," Maggie says. They're all smiles

"And if those two aren't sleeping together already, they will be soon," Dave adds.

"I sure hope so." I wave to them. Maggie and Shane becoming a couple warms my heart and makes me think about Dylan's invitation.

The ABBA song ends, and Star leads Woody over to us.

"Jenna!" Star says, excited. "We were just thinking. This is so much fun. We're going to host a dinner party for the old gang on Sunday. Right, Woody?"

"Sure, honey bun, that's a great idea," Woody recites dutifully. But his face tells me he's less than excited about hosting the "old gang."

"You'll come, right?" Star says. touching my arm. "And you too, Dave?"

"Sorry, twinkle toes. I'm heading back tomorrow. But Jenna would love to go. She was just telling me how she needs to be more social. Right, J?"

"Of course." I force a smile. I can't exactly say "No offense, Star, but the less time spent time with your philandering, abusive, future husband, the better."

The band starts playing David Bowie's "Let's Dance," and Dave grabs my hand. "Ooh, let's!"

Chapter 11
Super Sports

In the morning, Dave and I wake up late to find Martha making her famous ginger tea cure-all and a generous stack of fluffy pancakes. Dave holds the steaming cup of tea between his palms like a hibernating bear before swallowing the magic concoction and digging into his breakfast.

"I've never felt this awful," he moans.

"Really? I'm pretty sure I've seen you worse," I tease, enjoying my syrupy sweet meal.

"How late were you kids out?" Mom says.

"It wasn't the hour. It was the supersized nightcap Dave drank after we got home."

Dave tosses his napkin on the table. "Why didn't you stop me?"

Mom looks at him sympathetically as she clears his plate. "I'll pack you a thermos of tea for the road."

Dave rubs his temples. "You're the best."

I wish he could stay longer, but he has a business to run, and I have a murder to solve.

"Come on, party boy. We'd better get moving if you're going to catch the noon train." I drag his bags to the front door.

Dave stands up, and Mom hands him a thermos of tea.

"Thank you, Martha. You are a generous hostess. And thank you for raising my best friend." He kisses her on both cheeks.

"Now, don't be a stranger." Martha squeezes his shoulders affectionately and walks us to the door. She waves as we climb into my chilly car. Dave sinks into the passenger seat and slips on dark glasses to block out the "snow glare" as we pull away from the house.

"God, I hope this train has a smoother ride than the one up here," he says with a note of dread.

"I hate to tell you, but I think they're all the same."

Dave groans and closes his eyes behind his glasses. When we pull up to the station, we have ten minutes to spare. I blast the heat and let the motor run. I can't leave Dave on that godforsaken platform by himself, not in his condition.

"No offense hon, I had a great time, but I can't wait to get back to civilization," Dave says. "I need a mani-pedi. I honestly don't know how Martha manages to look so turned out when her self-care is DIY."

I laugh, already missing the way he grounds me. "No moving upstate for you, I guess."

He tips his glasses up. "Ab-so-lute-ly not."

In the distance, a train whistle sounds. Dave starts gathering his stuff together.

"I guess this is it," I sigh. "See you in a couple of months."

"Check in every day. And don't obsess over the case too much. You need balance in your life," Dave says, checking his shoulder bag and phone.

"Yes sir." I hand him the thermos full of tea.

"Ooh. And text me if that Dylan Connor calls you. He's

nothing like you described. You should definitely see more of him. All work and no play makes Jenna a dull girl."

"Don't worry, mother hen. I'll be fine."

"Au revoir, à la prochaine." Dave kisses my cheeks, grabs his luggage, and scurries across the platform and through the train's open doors. As usual, he leaves a hole behind him in the universe. As the train disappears, the emptiness swallows me.

Tapping my fingers on the steering wheel, I think about the case. I need evidence, and so far, the trophy lead hasn't panned out. What about the clothing the killer wore that night? Cece said nobody ever followed up on that. A professional would buy those items for one-time use. He'd have fake IDs and accounts that trace back to false identities. But an amateur might buy locally, maybe even use a credit card. There's only one place he would go—Super Sports. Martha took Tyler and me there every year to buy our gym gear.

Cece's warning echoes in my mind—don't do anything crazy. Stopping in a sporting goods store hardly qualifies as crazy.

I back up and turn toward the west side of town. Driving across the Scrublands, the road is empty, except for an SUV far behind me in the rearview mirror. As I cross the Winter Bridge, I look out the window. The ice is almost black on the deeper parts of the river. The hairs on my arm stand up as I pass the spot where Abby fell through. There are obvious patches where the ice is thinner and more dangerous. If only I could go back in time and warn her, save her.

Fifteen minutes later, I turn into a warren of warehouses. The Super Sports hasn't changed much—no-nonsense metal doors with a front window that would make a New York window dresser weep in despair. Cardboard figures are on display dressed in primary colors. A modern camera system has been installed over the front door. Inside, only a few shoppers are milling among the racks and bargain bins. And there are cameras on the checkout counter, so that's promising. I pass rows of identical shirts, trousers, windbreakers, and gym shoes stacked on towers of boxes. Every few feet, a bright yellow sign reads: *Sale!* I walk past the racks to the manager's office and knock on the door. Band music is playing, followed by a roaring cheer. The sound stops as a balding man dressed in a flashy tracksuit opens the door. He's well-muscled with broad shoulders and sporting a heavy gold necklace and rhinestone-encrusted tennis shoes. Behind him, a shelf displays assorted trophies, a championship ring in a case, and framed pictures of famous athletes. On his computer screen, a football game is frozen.

"Can I help you?" he says, distracted.

"Sorry to bother you. I'm from Bell River PD. Are you the manager?"

"The owner," he says. "Jim Rogers, call me Jimmy."

"Can I ask you some questions about your camera system?"

"You're a detective?" Jimmy's eyebrows rise in interest.

"The Bell River PD sent me," I say, fibbing ever so slightly.

"Uh-huh." He bobs his head fast as if he understands. "What's this about?"

"A crime committed four years ago."

"You think Super Sports' cameras got a shot of the perp?"

Now I know why he's excited—he's a crime buff.

"That's very astute of you, Jimmy. That's exactly right."

Jimmy grins, his sports game forgotten. "I always told my wife. One of these days, honey, the cops are gonna need me."

"Well, you're right. Your cameras look modern. Did you upgrade from an older system?"

"Sure did, last year. Before that, we used CCTV."

Just my luck. Those systems dump after six months.

"I see. Then I guess you don't have the footage—"

"Are you kidding? I save everything on flash drives." He winks. "Follow me."

Jimmy leads me out the back door to the storage warehouse just behind the store. He slides the door open and runs a hand along the dated binders on a shelf. "So what're we looking for?"

I point to the binder that corresponds to the year Coach Vitner was killed. Jimmy opens the file, revealing flash drives sealed in zipped pouches and organized by date. Jackpot!

"Can I take these?" I can't believe my luck.

"For your investigation? Sure! What about receipts? They always need receipts on those *CSI* shows. My bookkeeper will be back on Monday. Same year?"

"Yes! That would be great." I pull a pen and notepad from my bag. "These are the clothing brands and sizes we're searching for and the date range."

"You got it." He takes the paper from me.

"And Jimmy, I'd appreciate it if you only discussed the case with me and on a need-to-know basis."

"Of course," Jimmy says, excited. There's a flurry of wings as something flies up in the rafters. "Don't mind the pigeons. If there's a receipt, we'll find it."

Back at my car, I tuck the binder away to keep the flash drives safe for the ride to town. The road is empty, with powdery flurries of snow blowing across the road. Only an hour has passed, but the ice floats under the Winter Bridge have already shifted. I shiver with the memory of how dangerous that ice can be, constantly changing. You can't trust it. Abigail found that out on the day she died.

"Call Maggie," I tell Siri. After a couple of rings, she picks up.

"Wassup?" she says, distracted. The sound of shuffling paper comes through the phone speaker.

"Guess what I just found?" I say excited.

"No idea."

"The manager of Super Sports kept CCTV tapes—for decades. He downloaded the footage onto flash drives."

"Oh, good God! Really? We'll need special equipment—" The line cuts out with a static buzz.

"Maggie? Are you there?" I'm at that weird spot by the river. Cell service was always patchy out here, where the tree branches reach toward the sky like gnarled fingers and the wind blows through the hollow of the riverbank. "Maggie? Can you hear me?" I shout over the whistling wind. "Maggie!" I'm about to give up when her voice cuts back in.

"Shane'll have what we need. Meet me at his shop in an hour?"

"Great. See you then." I feel a sense of triumph. Maybe there's a clue to Coach Vitner's murder on the tapes. I glance in the rearview mirror. About a mile back is a big, black SUV. It looks exactly like the SUV I noticed earlier.

Cece's warning comes back to me. If Tyler's innocent, then the Bell River murderer could be anywhere—or anyone. Okay, now I'm being paranoid. That driver was probably just out shopping. As Martha would say, the world doesn't revolve around you, Jenna.

But before I can laugh it off, the SUV speeds up behind me. I drift to the right lane to make space, but instead of passing, the jerk tailgates me. When I try to get a look inside, the windows are tinted, making the driver invisible. The road narrows as we cross the Winter Bridge. Then, with a thud, the SUV taps my bumper. What the—

I blast my horn, frustrated. What's this guy doing? The road spanning the river is barely two lanes, and the cement is slippery, with a light crusting of ice from the damp air—my back tires swerve, fishtailing across the bridge. Then, the whole car slips off the road, tires spinning in the snow before finding purchase and bumping back onto the pavement. I blast the horn again in frustration.

As soon as we're over the bridge, the SUV tears out and passes me, shooting ahead toward the intersection that leads to town. Probably just some bored, redneck jerks looking for trouble. My blood is boiling, but instead of launching into road rage, I take a few controlled breaths. At least it's over.

Then, up ahead, there's a roaring screech. The SUV does a donut and comes to a jolting stop, blocking the road. The driver revs the engine menacingly, and I notice for the first time that the license plate is blacked out.

"No way!" I say aloud. I guess I wasn't paranoid enough.

I roll to a stop, keeping my distance. The engine revs again. Then, the driver's side window slides down, and a gloved hand emerges.

Is that a gun?

There's a loud pop, followed by a pinging sound. A crack appears in the center of my windshield. I slam my car in reverse and press my foot hard on the gas. The car lurches backward, bucking as I look over my shoulder and back up at high speed. There's another popping sound as the driver of the SUV shoots again. Then, the hulking black SUV lurches forward. I floor it backward over the Winter Bridge, swerving precariously, almost tumbling off the edge and down the bank into the frozen river. As I descend the far side of the bridge, the incline and ice work in my favor, whipping the car around in a crazy J-turn, reversing my direction. I change gears to drive and punch the accelerator as the SUV closes in, slamming into my bumper. My car jolts forward. The physics of this duel is a nightmare. My car can't do more than 100 miles per hour, and that SUV can easily do much more. My only advantage is my size; the SUV is heavier, so gravity isn't this guy's friend.

I calculate my chances of reaching the mall before this creep drives me off the road. The odds are not good. Then I remember something. There's a turn up ahead. I pray my memory is accurate. I don't want the SUV to know what I'm up to. So I tear down the road, veering slightly left as if fleeing to the mall. Then I take a hard right, almost swerving into a ditch, and tear up the side road at full speed.

In the rearview mirror, the SUV overshoots the road. If this jerk wants to continue the chase, he'll have to double back.

"Take that, you dumbass!" I yell, pounding the steering wheel.

Sure enough, up ahead is McCabe's Bar and Grill, the roadside dive where kids used to go to buy pot, or at least that was the rumor at school. I went there myself a few times with a fake ID. The parking lot is filled with cars and trucks lined side by side. I turn into the parking lot at high speed, barely able to control my car. Then I slam on the brakes and slide between a monster truck and a mega jeep, effectively disappearing.

The black SUV speeds past, disappearing out of sight. I'm breathing hard as I grab the binder full of flash drives, shove it in my backpack, and head into McCabe's. I need to lay low until it's time to meet Maggie.

McCabe's Bar and Grill hasn't changed. The vibe is blue-collar workers and a few bikers passing through town. The same wooden tables I remember are covered in drink stains and scattered cardboard coasters printed with a thirty-year-old graphic of a four-leaf clover on a beer stein.

In the center of the bar is a full-sized pool table with three guys deep in play. As I walk by, they notice me, big guys wearing jeans, T-shirts, and heavy work boots. The tallest of the three has long red hair and a bushy beard. He grins at me like the party just arrived. I'd consider it a compliment if I weren't the only woman in the place.

McCabe's has always been rough. When I was a teenager, the place was exciting, but now I notice things my younger self didn't see: the threadbare carpet, grimy windows, and chipped paint. Still, being in a place filled with burly guys is a relief after being chased by the SUV from Hell.

On the edge of the pool table is a line of quarters placed by people waiting for their turn to play. I head to the long bar decorated with neon Budweiser signs. On the far end, two guys in leather jackets eat burgers and fries.

With relief, I sit down on a tall, padded stool and set my backpack down. My nerves are shot. I check my phone. I've got forty minutes to kill before Maggie shows up at C&C. The bartender is an older guy with a ponytail and pockmarked skin. I signal him, and he saunters over with a quizzical expression and a bar towel draped over his shoulder. Before I can open my mouth, I recognize a smooth, familiar voice.

"I'm buying." Dylan Connor leans on the bar. He looks different than he did last night. His short brown hair is tousled and unruly. His warm eyes are slightly amused. He's wearing a royal blue polo shirt paired with a leather flight jacket with the sleeves pushed up and a braided leather bracelet with a dog-shaped charm hanging around his wrist.

"What are you doing here?" I say, surprised.

Dylan nods toward the pool game. "I'm embarrassed to tell you."

"Don't be. I can take it." I smile.

"Promise not to laugh?"

"Promise."

"See that crew over there playing pool?"

I look over at the pool game. The giant red-haired guy sees Dylan with me and shakes his head like he's already lost.

"I see them," I say.

"We were all Eagle Scouts. It's my second reunion in two days."

"Eagle Scouts? Are you serious?" I cover my mouth to stop laughing.

"Scout's honor." Dylan holds up two fingers. "You promised not to laugh."

"I should have known." I point to his bracelet. "What's this?"

"It's a Gray Wolf. Dad and I started a charity to benefit endangered species in New York state. Wolves are incredibly misunderstood. Have you ever seen one?"

"Coyotes, yes. But never a wolf." I'm impressed. Dylan may be rich, but he's also generous and cares about animals.

Dylan slides onto the seat next to mine. "So, what brings you here, Jenna?"

"I was just run off the road by some nut job. Road rage."

"Are you okay?" His eyes bulge with concern.

"Fine. I just stopped in to calm my nerves and kill some time before I meet up with Maggie."

"Let's get you a drink." Dylan signals the bartender, who pulls a bottle of vodka from a fridge and pours two glasses on the rocks. He pushes the glass over to Dylan, who slips him a few bills. A wisp of vapor floats off the ice.

Dylan clinks his glass against mine. "To old friends meeting again."

"To old friends." I drink. The taste is heavenly. Hot and cold simultaneously.

"I'm glad we ran into each other." He leans forward.

There's that chemistry again. It feels like I'm on the top of a roller coaster about to drop. I glance away, suddenly feeling nervous to meet his gaze.

One of Dylan's friends motions for him. He's up next.

"Looks like your turn." I finish my shot, and a warm ease flows through my body.

"Do you play?" Dylan says, running a finger along the rim of his glass.

"Sure. But it's been a while."

"Well, come on, Stack. Let's see what you got." He takes my hand, and a jolt of electricity passes through our fingertips. Then he pulls me gently toward the table.

"Just a sec." I grab my backpack and follow. His friends gawk at me as I take off my jacket and lay it over the bag.

"Dan, Billy, and Randy, this is Jenna."

"Hey, Jenna," the guys say, glancing at each other.

"No jokes about Eagle Scouts." Dylan grins.

"Never," Billy says.

Dan, the guy with the beard, grins. But this time, his eyes stay down. I guess Dylan is the leader of the pack.

"This one should be perfect." Dylan picks up a pool cue, measuring the stick against my height. He takes my hand and suggestively wraps my fingers around the shaft.

I feel the weight of the cue and test the balance. When was the last time I played pool? Oh yeah, every damn day of my life all through college. My dad taught me when I was little and took me to play once a week. I've always had a knack for the game.

Dylan racks the balls, carefully alternating stripes and solids with the eight-ball in the middle. Well, that is gentlemanly of him. Sometimes, when guys think you don't know the rules, they rack the balls without alternating so they can set up their future shots. Looks like Dylan Connor is an honest player. When the balls are centered, he chalks his cue. Then he gestures for me to break the rack. Thoughtful.

I line up my shot and scatter the balls without sinking anything—no need to tip these guys off. Dan, Billy, and Randy smile smugly in the corner.

"Ten in the corner pocket." Dylan sets up his shot, sinks the ball quickly, and makes a run on the stripes. Three balls later, it's my turn again.

"Seven in the side pocket?" I say, feigning self-doubt.

Dylan smiles patiently. "Do you know English?"

He's referring to putting a spin on the ball, which I'll need to do to make the shot. But I'm not about to give myself away.

"It's my first language," I answer.

Dan, Billy, and Randy exchange glances and smirks.

"No, I mean, do you know how to spin the ball? Here. Let me show you." Dylan moves in close to me and places my fingers on the cue. Then he presses his body against mine and covers my hands. My pulse quickens as he points the cue at a downward angle. The heat of his body is distracting. My breath catches in my throat.

"Now, you need to be light-handed. No follow-through if you want the ball to snap back." He lets go and stands back, confident. Is it the game he thinks he's mastered or me?

"Like this?" I take the shot—the seven ball spins and drops into the pocket. Then the cue ball snaps back and side pockets the two-ball before angling across the table to clip the three and five balls into the corner pocket. With the solids cleared, I sink the eight-ball.

Dan, Billy, and Randy watch, thunderstruck.

"Jenna Stack, you played me," Dylan says, a stunned look on his face.

"Did I?" I rack my cue and smile sweetly. "Listen, this has been fun, but I have to meet Maggie." I pull on my coat, sling the back-pack over my shoulder, and wave to the guys. "Thanks for letting me interrupt your play."

"I'll walk you out," Dylan offers.

Outside, I scan the parking lot. One of the trucks hiding my car has gone, but thankfully, there's no black SUV waiting. I unlock my car and throw my pack on the passenger seat.

"Thanks for the drink." I look up at him.

Another spark passes between us. I must admit—Dylan is sexy as hell, and I'm starting to like him. He's grown up since high school—still confident and charming, but his ego doesn't bruise so easily anymore.

Suddenly, he grows serious. That hint of sadness flashes across his eyes—the thing I never really understood as a kid. He slips a finger under my jacket and pulls me closer.

"I didn't get to tell you this last night, Jenna, but I want you to know," he says gently, "I'm really sorry about what happened to your brother."

The blood rushes to my face. "I thought you—"

"What?"

"You don't blame him?" The words seem to dissolve in the cold air.

"God, no. The night the coach was killed, I was with Dad in NYC at a political event. I was shocked when I got back and heard what happened. I know there was evidence, but I still find it hard to believe."

"Thanks, Dylan. That means a lot."

He takes my hand and looks at me with longing. "Listen, Jenna—"

"I have to go." The words blurt out of my mouth. "Maggie's waiting."

The pull between us is formidable, and the urge to convince

Dylan of Tyler's innocence is intense. But right now, I need to focus on solving the case.

I unlock the car and slip into the driver's seat.

"I also forgot to get your number last night." Dylan smiles. "Is it still okay for me to call you?"

I feel the heat rise in my cheeks. "I'd like that."

We exchange numbers, and I pull onto the icy road, still warm from our encounter.

Chapter 12
Suspect

For the past two hours, I've been scanning the Super Sports footage on top speed in Shane's office at The Curiosities & Comics Emporium while Maggie helps him organize a recent bulk purchase of old comics. The sound of them giggling and squealing with delight wafts in from the other room as they unpack and inspect each treasure.

I decided not to share my harrowing experience with the black SUV or my encounter with Dylan. I don't want to worry them. And while I'm grateful for the use of Shane's media equipment, I'm not in the mood to chat.

The *Star Trek* red alert doorbell chimes, and I hear a muffled exchange. Maggie steps into the office.

"No luck?"

"Nope. I'm up to the day of the murder. Do you think I should go further back?"

Shane appears holding a pizza box. The smell of tomatoes and melted cheese fills the air.

"Why don't you take a break and eat something with us?" he suggests.

"In a minute. I just want to finish this day—"

I hit stop, not believing my eyes. Could it be? I rewind the tape. There they are on the sales counter: ski mask, hoodie, tennis shoes. I rewind further back and gesture to Maggie and Shane. "Come look."

I hit play and we all watch a man wearing a baseball hat low over his eyes and a combat jacket with a double cobra on the back approach the register. He drops a ski mask, hoodie, and trainers on the counter, pays cash, and walks out.

"What do you think?" I ask hopefully.

"They match the items the killer tossed," Maggie agrees.

"Yeah, but those are common purchases from a sporting goods store, right?" Shane says.

"But look." Maggie points to the onscreen time code. "Three o'clock on the day of the murder. That's a pretty big coincidence."

"There's no such thing as coincidence." I shake my head. "And if it is the killer, this shows premeditation."

I play the section of tape twice more as the three of us hunch over the screen trying to catch a glimpse of the man's face.

"There. Freeze!" Maggie shouts.

We all lean in to inspect a grainy black-and-white still image of the man's whole body in profile as he approaches the counter. He appears to be around the same height as Tyler, but he's heavier, more muscular, and his chin is softer.

My heart feels like it might explode in my chest.

"That's definitely not Tyler," Maggie confirms what I'm thinking.

I take out my phone and carefully record the sequence, then text it to my friend Nadir.

Me: *Crucial evidence. Do whatever you geniuses do to store, save, protect.*

I spin around in my chair. Maggie and Shane are smiling with their arms wrapped around each other's waists.

"I can put the original in my safe," Shane offers.

"That'd be great. Thanks."

"Then pizza?" He eyes the unopened box.

I'm too pumped up with adrenaline to eat.

"You two go ahead. I need to show this to Detective Myers right away."

Cece and Boomer live just around the corner from the bistro. Driving along, looking for their address, I'm reminded how much Bell River has changed. Half the properties are empty and deteriorating. Most of the streetlights are out, and the asphalt is full of potholes. The wind whips snow flurries off the ground, and even in my heated car, I feel chilled and on edge.

Dotted among the neglect are a few tidy, well-kept houses with a welcoming glow in their windows. The Myers home is one of these hopeful beacons, complete with twinkling holiday lights.

As I pull to the gloomy curb, a dark SUV turns onto the street and heads toward me. There's no front license plate, and I can't see inside. Fear shoots up my spine. As I'm weighing my options, the car passes by. A harried-looking woman sits behind the wheel. A few houses down, she pulls over. A young boy in a soccer uniform jumps out and races up to a dimly lit home.

I shake off the scare, lock up my car, and before I reach the front door, Boomer and Cece appear on their porch.

"Now, you enjoy that cassoulet, and I'll be home later," Boomer coos.

Cece nods and kisses him softly. I feel awkward witnessing such a private moment, so I slow my pace. As Boomer turns to leave, they notice me.

"Hi, Jenna."

"Hey Boomer. Going out?"

"Saturday night dinner shift. Best night of the week." He smiles and heads to the sidewalk.

I watch Boomer walk down the street, a happy man with a loving wife, off to a job and business he loves. If Cece gets fired because of me and they have to move, I'll never forgive myself. We've got to find a way to get rid of Sheriff Wade.

"So you've got something?" Cece interrupts my thoughts, all business.

"I do." I hope she shares my confidence once she sees the flash drives.

The inside of the Myers house matches the outside. It's warm and welcoming, with a fire burning and cozy, colorful furniture.

Cece leads me to the kitchen, which smells like smoked meat and garlic. My stomach reminds me it's been hours since breakfast with Martha and Dave.

A large casserole dish sits on the stove, with an even larger cat sniffing at the rim.

"Knock that off, Sam," she scolds the cat, and it jumps to the floor.

"I'm really sorry to interrupt your evening, Detective Myers."

She shrugs and stirs the delicious-smelling concoction. "I tell Boomer not to bother. I can make a salad or scramble up some eggs."

"It smells great. You're so lucky—"

"Take a seat," she interrupts me, making it clear she let me in her home on a Saturday night for police business, not girl talk.

Then she hands me an open bottle of cabernet and two glasses. "As long as you're here, pour me a glass and help yourself if you'd like. Then tell me what you've found."

We settle in at the kitchen table and I walk her through my day. I tell her about Jimmy at Super Sports and my encounter with the SUV. She peppers me with a few questions, like, "Did you see the driver? Were there any identifying dents or scratches on the SUV?" But mostly, she just listens, sips her wine, and pets the cat.

When I get to the part about reviewing the CCTV flash drives at Shane's shop, I take out my phone, queue up the footage of the mystery man at the cash register, and hand it to her.

"I know it's grainy but..."

The cat rearranges itself on the tabletop, and I scratch behind its fluffy ears.

She watches the sequence several times before asking, "The original is secure?"

I nod. "Shane put it in his safe."

"And you have backup copies?"

"Yes." I wait, but she doesn't offer anything more. "So, what do you think?"

She hands me back the phone.

"I think this is a solid lead. Good work."

Relief and excitement wash over me, followed by a sense of pride in a job well done. I imagine this must be what Boomer feels like every night at the bistro.

"First thing Monday, we go see Jimmy about the receipt," she adds, a flash of excitement in her eyes.

"Great." I stand up and gather my things.

"In the meanwhile, have you ever had cassoulet?"

Chapter 13
Dinner Party Disaster

Beyond the edge of town, there are no streetlights. Tall snowbanks line the sides of the narrow roads, and the only sound is my noisy car. I crack the window and drink in the crisp, clean air and moonlit landscape, following my navigation app through twists and turns past infrequent homes set back from the road. I'm contemplating how peaceful it is when a coyote howls and another replies. No. I don't think I'd like living way out here. Too isolated.

The app sends me down a dead-end road to an enormous set of gates emblazoned with a gold W. There's a camera and an inter-com. Before I push the button to speak, the stately gates part. I wave and cruise my clunker up the long, curved driveway. The house up ahead is a Greek revival mansion with tall white columns and a peaked roof. This doesn't really seem like Star somehow. When we used to talk about where we wanted to live in the future, she always used to say a cottage or farmhouse, not this type of pretentious place.

At the top of the hill, the driveway splits. I veer left and end up along the side of the house. There are no other cars around, not even Star's Chrysler. I grab the bouquet I picked up at the grocery mart on my way out of town and check my watch. I'm ten minutes late. Am I the first? As I climb the driveway, the tall white columns come into view. A teenage valet waits on the steps dressed in a navy dress coat, scrolling through his phone. Is that little Freddy Wade, Woody's cousin? He barely notices me as I walk past him to the front door.

I ring the bell. The first few notes of the "Star-Spangled Banner" ring out. Funny, I don't remember Woody being particularly patriotic in high school. Now everything seems to be about his all-American image.

Star answers the door wearing white slacks and a fluffy white sweater. Her hair is perfectly curled, and a set of pearls rests at her throat. She'll make an amazing political wife, but it doesn't feel right somehow. She was always more of a hippie type, reading poetry and volunteering her time. She called twice today to discuss the dinner menu—beet and fennel salad, salmon with roasted vegetables, and pecan chocolate crumble with homemade vanilla ice cream. Yet there isn't a speck of proof that she's been cooking on her pristine outfit.

"Jenna! I'm so glad you came." She throws her arms around me warmly.

"For the hostess." I present her with a colorful bouquet of roses, chrysanthemums, and freesia.

"They're gorgeous, thank you." She points to a low row of cubbies filled with shoes, including Maggie's familiar Dr. Martens. Above that are hooks for purses and coats. So, I guess everyone else got the valet parking memo. As I take off my jacket, I suddenly feel underdressed in jeans, with a blouse and cardigan.

"I didn't know this was going to be fancy," I say.

Star points to my feet. "Shoes off," she whispers. "Woody has rules."

I hang up my bag, tug off my snow boots. Only then do I realize I'm wearing one white and one striped, pink sock. The tile floor is cold through the thin cotton fabric.

Woody bounds down the steps, takes a look at me, and points to the hooks.

"I'll need your keys." He holds out his hand without saying hello.

Star looks ill, clutching the bouquet of flowers to her chest. She nods at me, terror in her eyes.

"Why on Earth do you want my keys?" I say. "I'm parked around the—"

"I saw that. There's a valet system here, Jenna," Woody says tightly. "Freddy!"

Freddy comes running inside. "Yes, Woody?"

"Go find Miss Stack's car and park it with the others."

I don't love the idea of surrendering my keys. But I don't want to start the evening with a confrontation, so I drop them in Woody's hand. He throws the keys to his nephew. Then his phone buzzes. He looks at the screen, distracted. "I gotta take this call, babe."

As he disappears around the corner, Star lets out her breath and leads me into the living room.

"Jenna's here," Shane says, dressed in a velvet blazer over a HAL 9000 T-shirt. He gives me a hug as Maggie slides beside me. She's looking cute, with her hair tied up in fuzzy pom poms, wearing a black, button-down jumper dress over a hot pink long-sleeved shirt and striped tights.

"I think parking is a big deal around her," Maggie whispers. "Something about ruining the view. There was an email."

"I guess I missed it," I say under my breath. "What view?"

Maggie shrugs and drinks her wine.

Looking around the living room, I see why it's a shoes-off

household. From the floors to the furniture to the throw pillows, everything in the house has the same austere palette. Candles, coasters, and even the artwork on the walls are shades of ivory, birch, and sand.

"Let me show you around." Star takes me for a quick tour of the ground floor.

"Woody says color makes a person seem radical," Star says. "So, the den is toasted pecan. The kitchen is winter white." She opens a door. "The bathroom is cream, the dining room is almond, and" — she stops in front of a large wooden door— "Woody's office is camel, but it's off-limits."

I'm struck by how different this home is from Cece's. The former is grand but rigid and impersonal, while the latter feels cozy and inviting—full of love.

"You used to love color," I point out, remembering the beaded curtains and bright throw pillows in Star's childhood bedroom.

"I still do, but we all have to make sacrifices," Star says.

We move on to the kitchen, which gleams with white marble countertops and stainless-steel appliances. Salmon is marinating in a glass pan on the counter. Both ovens are on, and the rich smell of chocolate and roasted nuts fills the air.

I peek into what most people would call a mudroom and spy an exact duplicate of Star's outfit, waiting neatly on a hanger.

She blushes. "Just in case."

A maid walks in with a tray of folded napkins. She's short and muscular with a bright smile. She scoops the flowers from Star's hands, snips the stems, and places them in a vase.

"Thank you, Edna," Star says. "Jenna, meet Edna, my sous chef for the evening."

We shake hands.

"Go ahead with your guests, Miss Star," Edna says. "Everything's under control here."

There's an engine roar and a flash of lights outside. From the window, we see a dark sedan pull up to Freddy the valet. Star claps her hands excitedly. "Oh, good. That's everyone."

We join the others just as Dylan Connor walks through the front door, wearing jeans and a faded Cornell University sweatshirt under a leather jacket. He's carrying a clean, folded T-shirt over one arm. His hair is unruly, and there's a black smudge on his cheek. "Sorry, I'm late. Mrs. Sherman's water heater blew."

He hands Star a bottle of wine.

She looks at the label, and her eyes grow wide. "Oh my gosh, you shouldn't have."

Dylan grins. "Least I could do."

"Don't you have people for that?" Woody sneers, arms crossed.

"Yes, but Mrs. Sherman's been alone since her husband died. She was Dad's English teacher. I felt like I should at least stop by. Forgive me?"

"Of course, I do." Star beams. "We're happy you could join us."

"Just give me a minute to clean up," he says as he heads to the bathroom.

I look down at my mismatched socks and then back at Star.

"You didn't tell me Dylan would be here," I whisper.

"I must have forgotten to mention it." She raises an eyebrow and smiles.

I smooth my messy ponytail. I hate to admit it, but if I'd known Dylan was coming, I'd have put on a little makeup.

The dinner table is set beautifully in all-white linen, pale roses, and bone China, with cut-crystal glasses. Star is a natural hostess, quietly communicating with Edna so that things run smoothly as she serves the courses, one after another, cooked to perfection. Guests ooh and aah over the elegant presentation and delicious flavors. Dylan sits directly across from me, in a fresh, black T-shirt, his cheeks flushed and his eyes warm and magnetic. Everyone is behaving like it's a perfectly normal evening with friends, but I'm having an out-of-body experience. People overuse the word surreal to describe unusual situations. But it's the only word I can think of for this bizarre scene. If you'd told me eight years ago that Star and Woody would become a couple or Dylan Connor would turn out to be a nice guy, I wouldn't have believed it. Maggie and Shane's budding romance doesn't surprise me (I saw that coming in high school), and Woody's childish, spoiled brat attitude is exactly the same. He may be dressed in nice clothing, but he's the same impatient, aggressive jock underneath. When the conversation is about Woody, he's happy and engaged, but the moment it switches to somebody else's life or accomplishments, he's bored and impatient. In fact, all evening long, Star has been trying to keep the chit-chat flowing while Woody finds ways to turn the spotlight back on himself.

"So, then I said to the senator, sure, I'll run for Congress, but it'll cost you." Woody laughs at his own joke. Then his phone buzzes. He texts back quickly and tucks it away.

Edna moves around the table, intuitively filling water glasses and taking plates away. She is a study in selflessness in contrast to Woody's self-involvement.

"You know," Star says. "Maggie works at the police station—"

"I know, I know," Woody says. "Dad told me she does some filing."

"Actually, I'm an evidence technician." Maggie's eyes flash with anger, but she has too much self-control to argue. Instead, she sips her wine and watches him as if he's an animal at the zoo.

"Filing is filing, am I right? Now, my major was a toss-up, politics versus law. But then I addressed the Rotary Club, and I got a standing ovation. They loved my five-point plan."

Star tries again. "Did you know Shane has a new store?"

"Good for you, Buckskin. Have you seen my collection? I've got an autographed O.J. Simpson football. I met Tom Brady in Vegas, and he signed a menu for me. Man, his wife was hot."

"That's right, you used to call me Buckskin because of the movie..." Shane says remembering the slight. Maggie reaches for his hand and squeezes.

Woody's phone buzzes again. He looks at the screen and grins before sending out another reply. Then he puts his phone on the table where he can keep an eye on it.

I sip some of the expensive wine Dylan brought. After an evening with Woody, it's clear the kind of Congressman he will be —a bad one. I can safely say that Star is making a huge mistake. I don't know how to convince her to leave this idiot, but if she doesn't, her life will be a nightmare. Maybe not today, and maybe not tomorrow, but someday.

As we all finish our salmon, Edna brings out an exquisite pecan chocolate crumble. Woody ignores her as if she doesn't exist and turns to Dylan.

"So, your dad really thinks I can go all the way?" Woody says.

Up until now, Dylan has been quiet and laid back. He sets his spoon down and looks at Woody. I get the feeling he's answered some version of this question more than once.

"You know my dad, he's a shrewd businessman. He wouldn't contribute to your campaign if he didn't think you could win. But remember, a career in politics is about service, Woody."

"Yeah, sure...service." Woody smirks. "I couldn't agree more."

I only saw Dylan's dad once from afar at a football game, but everyone in school knew he was a successful Manhattan attorney who owned a lot of property in the area.

"Mr. Connor has been very generous," Star offers proudly. "Jenna, we haven't heard a peep from you. How's your internship going?"

"Great. Maggie is a genius at forensics. And Cece is by the book, but she's brilliant."

"That's weird," Woody comments, scooping a spoonful of crumble into his mouth.

"What do you mean, hon?" Star says sweetly.

"That you call your boss Cece?" He looks at me. "From what I hear, you two got into trouble."

I take a bite of dessert. and try to count to ten. I make it to five.

"Well, if you mean arresting your cousins?" I meet his eyes. "That was *good* trouble."

"Harassing innocent people? Come on, Jenna."

"Jay and Stan Spar are hardly innocent."

"And Cece is helping Jenna with Tyler's case," Star says, trying to relieve the tension.

Maggie kicks me under the table. I probably shouldn't have mentioned that fact to Star.

"Tyler?" Woody scowls. "That case is long closed. The only thing left for Tyler Stack is to serve his time."

"Come on, Woody," Dylan says. "You're going too far."

Heat rises along the back of my neck as I stare at Woody's smug expression.

"Detective Myers is mentoring Jenna," Maggie says casually. "We discuss all sorts of cases. And everyone calls her Cece. Right, Jenna?"

"But there's new evidence," Star pushes. "Evidence that could clear Tyler."

Shane freezes with his spoon halfway to his mouth. Maggie's eyes go wide. I can't quite remember what I said to Star. Oh yeah, that I visited Jimmy at the Super Sports.

"Evidence Dad missed?" Woody snaps. "I seriously doubt that's even possible."

"Your father is a wonderful sheriff, hon. But it was a long time ago, and nobody's perfect."

Woody's jaw clenches. He glares at Star, and the room fills with tension.

"You know, Star, ever since your friend here got back in town, you've been more idiotic than usual. Why don't you just stick to cooking?"

"Woody!" Dylan glares at him. "That's out of line."

Just then, Woody's phone rings. Everyone can see the words emblazoned on the screen—Peyton Honeycutt. He grabs the phone and stalks out of the room.

Star is mortified. Her cheeks blaze red.

"Let me help in the kitchen." I grab her hand and pull her into the stark white kitchen.

Edna's expression is tense. It's clear she's seen this all before. She points to a stainless-steel trashcan with a foot pedal and pops the lid open. There, sitting on the top of the trash, is the bouquet I brought.

"I'm sorry, Miss Star. I couldn't stop him," she says. "I'll clear the dessert plates."

Edna tactfully disappears.

Star looks at the flowers. "Oh Jenna, I'm sorry He's just so... particular about things. And he has a terrible temper."

I lean against the counter. "What about Peyton? How long has that been going on?"

"He always says it's nothing." She grabs a paper towel and dabs at her eyes. "That they're just friends."

"Listen, Star. I don't want to have to say this, but Woody is a controlling, abusive jerk. I'm worried about you.

"Star!" Woody shouts from the other room. "Your friends are leaving!"

Maggie and Shane are slipping on their shoes at the front door. Everyone is being careful, walking on eggshells.

"Dinner was delicious," Maggie says. "Thank you."

Star hugs them goodbye and they walk out hand in hand. Maggie and I will have plenty to talk about at work tomorrow.

"I'm going to, um, split, too," Dylan seems rattled as he hugs Star. "Thanks for a great meal."

Star smiles faintly. Then she walks toward Woody's office. The way she moves tells me everything I need to know. She's scared, and I'm not leaving her.

Dylan leans close by my cheek and whispers, "Do you think I should stick around?"

"I can handle it," I say. "I'll make sure she's okay."

Dylan smiles. "Okay. Call me if you need me. And how about dinner at Boomer's this week? Just the two of us."

"That'd be nice." I feel a tingle of excitement and wonder if he feels it, too.

He kisses my cheek and walks out.

A moment later Freddy Wade peeks his head in the door. "Could you tell Woody I'm taking off soon? I gotta meet some friends."

"Sure, Freddy."

I collect myself and follow muffled voices down the hallway. The door to Woody's office is open. The room is painted a dreary shade of camel. In the center is a massive wooden desk beneath a taxidermized deer head. Sports trophies and pennants cover the walls. His O.J. Simpson football is on display in a glass display cabinet.

Woody stands over Star, his face red with anger.

"How dare you speak that way? In front of Dylan. His dad is

my biggest donor," he rages and squeezes her arm hard. By morning, the imprint of his fingers will blossom into bruises.

"You're hurting me!" Star tries pull away. "They're our friends, and—"

"If I can't control my own wife, how can I command *his* respect?"

"If you can't control your temper, you'll never earn anyone's respect," I say, leaning against the doorframe. Star seems surprised and embarrassed. Then I see something worse pass across her face. Fear—for me.

Woody looks at me like I'm a rodent that wandered into his home. As his rage is escalates, so does mine.

"You!" Woody spits. "What poison have you been filling her head with?" He lets Star go and walks toward me. He's six foot tall and 180 pounds. He used to be a linebacker, so he's cocksure of himself. I remember my self-defense training. Use his strength against him.

Woody lunges at me.

I dodge his fist, and he tumbles forward and lands hard on his knee. Then I assume a defensive stance. As he struggles to his feet, Star grabs his arm to try and stop him. He reacts by smacking her so hard with the back of his hand she crashes against the desk and falls to the ground, limp. The room goes completely still except for her whimpers.

Stunned, Woody watches me cross over to Star.

"I didn't mean to...is she okay?" Woody says gruffly.

Star looks up at me, tears in her eyes and mouths *help me*.

I pull her to her feet and position her behind me.

Woody blocks the office door. Slowly, I pull out my phone.

"Think, Woody, think! I'm an intern with the police department. I've got Cece on speed dial. There are witnesses to your behavior tonight. One more step and I'll create a mess even Stockade Wade can't fix for you. Think about your campaign."

He hesitates, eyes reflecting an animal cunning. Then his manner shifts from unbridled rage to a twisted, narcissistic version of contrition.

"I'm sorry, honey. I didn't mean to hurt you. But you shouldn't have grabbed me like that."

He reaches forward and I feel Star cringe behind me, her heart beating fast.

"One way or the other, I'm taking her with me. Your choice."

I hold up my phone—finger poised on the speed dial.

Woody steps away from the door.

"Jenna, she knows how I get. I don't mean it. Please hon, don't do this." He covers his face with his hands and starts sobbing. There's no way to tell if it's an act or not, and I don't care.

As I pull Star forward, she hesitates, but I tighten my grip on her hand.

"I'm not leaving you here, Star. Move. Now." The thought that I'm bullying Star to get her away from her abusive fiancé flashes in my mind. But I don't have time to worry about my tactics right now. I just need to get her out of here.

Edna is standing by the front door, packed and ready to leave. She has a no nonsense look on her face. In her hands are Star's purse, coat and shoes.

"Let me help you, Miss Star." She bundles her into her parka and shoes, then slips her purse over one arm.

"Great. If there's anything else, we'll come back for it." I'm grateful for Edna's help.

A wave of panic hits. My keys! Freddy had them. I scan the wall. There they are, looped on the same hook as my purse. Thank goodness. I grab my stuff and yank open the door. Star hesitates on the threshold as if frozen in place by the blast of cold air.

Suddenly, there's a loud thud as the office door flies open.

"Stop!" Remorseful Woody has disappeared, and angry Woody is back. He strides toward us, fists clutched.

"GO!" I push Star out the door.

Cool as ice, Edna pulls the door shut and locks it with her key. Then, with a quick snap of her wrist, she breaks the shaft off in the lock.

Woody bangs on the door as we run to my car and start the engine.

Edna picks up her bags and walks to a Toyota 4Runner waiting in the driveway.

"Ladies first," Andy Barnes says, taking his cap off. "Me and Edna go way back."

Edna waves. "Good luck, Miss Star."

We pull away, and Andy Barnes' 4Runner follows us all the way home.

"Is that Star Simonsen?" Annie Dupont calls out her window as I bundle Star into the house. Martha should be home by now, but one of her many jobs is babysitting, so who knows? I get Star upstairs to my room, take off her coat and shoes. By the time I hang up her things and turn around, she's disappeared.

"Star?" I scan the room and then I see her huddled under my old paisley comforter.

"How did I let myself get in this situation?" Tears stream down her face. Martha's cats Alex and Eliza saunter into the room. Like a pair of Geiger counters for snuggles, they both climb onto the comforter and nestle around Star.

"How we got here doesn't matter," I tell her. "What matters is what you're going to do next." Maybe that sounds like a fortune cookie, but it's the best I can do under the circumstances.

There's a light knock on the door. Martha peeks her head inside the room.

"Did I hear crying—Star?" She races to the bed and puts her arm around my despondent friend.

Star sputters out between sobs. "I m-miss my grandma."

"Of course you do, dear." Martha rocks her gently. "She was a wonderful woman. Now tell me what's happened while Jenna makes tea." Martha gives me "the look." A combination of this is serious, do the right thing, and don't make it worse.

Downstairs, high in a kitchen cupboard, I find the old raven-shaped teapot mom used when the Raymond Chandler Appreciation Society met at our house. The lid has been broken and glued back together, and there's a chip in the spout. But there's something reassuring about its memories and tenacity. It's the right choice for tonight.

I remake the couch into a bed for myself while the water boils. Then I take my time preparing the tea tray. I'm lucky to have such a caring mother and happy to lend her to a friend in need.

By the time I push open the bedroom door, Star has stopped crying. There's even a hint of defiance in her eyes.

"Star has made a plan," Mom tells me, giving my friend full credit for something that was undoubtedly a team effort.

"That's great." I set the heavy tray down on my old, scarred desk.

"I'm going to leave him," Star announces.

I wait for the rest of the plan but neither of them speaks up.

"Is that it? A one-step plan?" I say. Mom gives me the look again, so I take the tone down a notch. "I don't mean to be harsh. I'm sure Woody cares about you. But what about his image? I don't think he's going to react well to losing his trophy wife so close to the election."

"They aren't married yet, and the election is almost a year away," Martha says.

"I was telling Martha," Star explains, "that I've been helping a little with the campaign, and I've learned a lot. There's still plenty of time for Woody to pivot."

"But the billboards? I saw one on the way into town."

"Those are only local. Testers. They're due to come down soon anyway."

"This all sounds very rational, Star. But Woody isn't rational." I avoid Martha's gaze. Star needs to be realistic.

"He'll listen to me. If I can convince him that I'm leaving no matter what and it's best for the campaign that it happens now, I don't think he'll really care."

"And she's going to stay here, with us, for as long as she needs," Martha adds.

I'm not convinced things will go as smoothly as they think, but I'm glad Star is ready to make a change. I pour us each a cup of tea.

Star twists the ring off her finger and drops it on the tea tray. It spins in a loud circle and rolls to a stop. "I always hated that thing," she giggles.

"Leaving him is the brave thing to do," Martha says.

Star notices the old raven teapot and smiles as she accepts the cup.

"And I don't want to be a trophy wife. What was that thing Raymond Chandler said once? Oh yes. 'I certainly admire people who do things.'"

Chapter 14
Burned

Cece insisted we meet at the crack of dawn. The sky is still dark. The neighborhood is blanketed with snow and quiet, except for a lone Amazon truck delivering packages. As I wait on the curb, the air is sharp in my lungs, helping wake me up. When I left this morning, Star was sleeping peacefully, safe, and sound for the first time in a long time. Away from Woody, she's more like her old self, and getting stronger every hour. All she needs is some time.

Half past 6 a.m. to the minute, Cece pulls up in the squad car. I quickly slide into the passenger seat. Even though the heat is blasting, it's freezing as usual. I tap the vent. Is this damned thing even blowing hot air?

"Morning," Cece chirps and hands me a coffee.

"You read my mind." I inhale the welcome aroma.

"Jimmy Rogers is meeting us at the Super Sports." Cece turns onto the main road, heading for the store. "Says he found receipts for the month of the Vitner murder." She looks at me and nods her approval. "Good detective work, Stack."

I break into a big grin. "Thanks, ma'am."

"Praise where praise is due," she says, humming to herself, which for Cece is practically exuberant.

Sipping my coffee, I feel warm and happy, like I belong. This is why I wanted to become a detective. Sometimes, the world doesn't make much sense, but solving a case is like following a compass. There might be twists and turns, but there's only one answer, one destination.

Slowly, the road lights up as the sun rises. Snow has settled on the tree branches overnight. The sparkly flakes catch the light, and clumps drop to the ground as the temperature ticks up a notch. Up ahead is the Winter Bridge. As we cross, Cece nods toward the sign honoring Abigail Wade.

"You must have been, what, in high school when the drowning happened?"

"I'll never forget the day. I was at the library after class. They sent everyone home."

"I don't care for Sheriff Wade," she says. "But I'd never wish losing a child on anyone."

"They say Sheriff Wade was warned about the ice jam upriver. If he'd had the ice removed, Abby would still be alive."

"No wonder he's mean as a wolverine." Cece frowns as the river disappears behind us. "Now, about Jimmy Rogers. Is he reliable?"

"He's a cop fan with a filing system to rival Maggie's any day."

A ghost of a smile plays at the corner of Cece's lips. She coasts down a gentle slope and takes a turn toward the Super Sports. "Good, because we need—"

Her eyes lock onto the sky, and her jaw tightens. A cloud of thick black smoke roils over the flat roofs of the low industrial block just ahead.

"Oh no," I manage to say.

Cece switches on the police lights and presses her foot down on the accelerator. The car fishtails on the icy pavement and the siren blares as she grabs the radio and says in a commanding voice, "Ten-three emergency." She screeches around the final corner, gripping the wheel in one hand and the radio in the other. The car skids to a stop as we face an awful sight—a building engulfed in flames.

"What you got there, boss?" Officer Pete's voice crackles with static.

Cece leans back and shakes her head.

"The Super Sports is on fire."

Jimmy Rogers stands with his back to us, silhouetted against the most enormous fire I've ever seen. Bright orange flames leap from the roof of his store. I can see why the power of the fire hypnotizes arsonists. It's like a living thing, a roaring beast with flames devouring everything it touches. Jimmy alternates between frantically talking into his cell phone, pacing, holding his phone up to record the scene, and folding over in abject horror. The building is being consumed before our eyes. Smoke billows out of every vent, moving with intense volition, pouring over the gutter and down the walls. The front windows are already blackened, and the mannequins on display are human-shaped torches, bubbling and warping behind the still-intact glass.

Cece jumps out of the car before I can even open the door. Though I haven't known her long, I've learned to recognize the signs that she's under pressure. Her jaw is tight, her eyes locked on target. She's harnessing her energy like a gathering storm.

"Sir?" she says, approaching Jimmy. "Are you all right?"

Jimmy turns, face red and angry. He points at the building, working his jaw.

"What the hell!" he finally manages to say, voice breaking. He points at the inferno. "That's my goddamned life in there."

"Yes, sir, I know." Cece motions me to come over. Nodding toward Jimmy, she whispers, "Keep an eye on him. He's in shock."

"Jimmy? The fire department is coming, okay?" I say gently.

"I've been here twenty years! Who would do this?" He bends over, catching his breath.

"We're going to find out, sir," Cece says. "There will be evidence. There always is."

The blaring sound of sirens fills the air as two fire trucks and an ambulance turn around the corner and pull up beside the Super Sports. The firefighters jump off the truck and hook the hoses up to hydrants. Within moments, water is arcing onto the roof. But the building is too far gone. Nothing will stop the fire, only contain the flames so it doesn't spread through the entire industrial park.

Jimmy Rogers sinks onto the hood of his Volvo. Under his Nike tracksuit and parka, his shoulders shake, and he starts to cry. Anybody would crumble watching their whole world destroyed.

"Um, Jimmy?" I say as gently as possible. "Those receipts you were going to show us. Where are they?"

"The warehouse," he says, trying to pull himself together.

I walk to the side of the building. The warehouse is completely engulfed. The building is smaller, and the roof is already gone. As if on cue, the floor collapses in a shower of sparks.

I walk back to where Cece is talking on the radio.

Seeing the look in my eyes, she tells Pete, "I'll call you later."

I point to the half-crumbled smoking hole in the ground that was the warehouse. All my frustration swells up in a wave.

"The receipts are gone, b-burned up…" My eyes are stinging, but I refuse to cry.

"I know you were hoping those receipts would prove Tyler's innocence. But we don't know that for sure," Cece says reassuringly.

"But—"

She grabs my shoulders and looks me in the eyes. Something in Cece's expression calms me. She sees me. She shares my pain.

"Every case hits roadblocks, Jenna. We still have the tapes. And we will not stop investigating—not until we have the answers we're looking for. We keep going. Do you hear me?"

"I hear you," I say, feeling more centered.

"Now, finish your coffee while we wait for the fire chief." Cece gets back on the radio to Officer Pete while I watch the firemen work.

An hour later, the Eastmoor County fire chief walks over to Cece. He's a tall, ruddy man with a mustache, wearing a blue suit under a fire jacket. The fire is under control at this point, but his men are still spraying arcs of water onto the roof.

"Hey Cece, how's Boomer?" the chief says with a solemn look on his face. Unlike his men, he looks like he's been sitting at a desk, not fighting a fire. He has a Toughbook laptop tucked under his arm.

"Just fine, Mike. What do you have for me?"

"Well, this is preliminary, so don't quote me…" Mike glances at me.

"She's okay. Officer in training," Cece explains.

"Well, the fire started in the warehouse before moving to the main building. It looks like an accelerant was used."

"You think it's arson?" she says casually.

"That's what I'm thinking. We'll launch an investigation, but firebugs are hard to catch. Remember, you haven't heard from me...yet." Mike touches his hat and walks back to confer with his men.

Cece turns to me and crosses her arms, her expression thoughtful and severe.

"Well, Jenna, looks like somebody wants to shut this case down. So, what do we do?"

"We keep going," I say.

Chapter 15
Independence Day

I spend the rest of the day back in the evidence locker, sorting through boxes, trying not to think about the fact that potential physical evidence in Tyler's case just went up in smoke. It's frustrating, so listening to Maggie gush about her budding relationship with Shane is a welcome distraction. I try to stay positive and upbeat, particularly when he drops off a rose midday along with a collector's pack of *Beetlejuice* trading cards. Honestly, I'm happy for her, but my mind keeps going back to the fire and Tyler's case. Why go to all the trouble of burning the Super Sports down? Maybe it's a message, or maybe I'm getting close and whoever's behind all this is scared.

By the time we clock out, all I want is a hot shower and some carbs. Maggie heads for Shane's shop to watch a rare anime movie, while I get in my clunker and head home. Maybe Mom and Star will be up for ordering a pizza.

The moment I step through the front door, I realize my plans are about to change drastically.

Star is slouched on the couch with her head in her hands.

Martha is pacing the room, her brow wrinkled. "Now dear, life is full of curveballs."

"What's going on?' I put my shoulder bag down and hang up my jacket.

"Oh, good," Mom says. "You're home." She sits next to Star and places an encouraging hand on her back. "Tell Jenna what's happened."

Star shakes her head. "I'm so embarrassed."

I perch on a chair across from them, "Are you kidding? You never have to be embarrassed in front of us. Right, Mom?"

"That's right." She smiles at me. "Go ahead, dear."

Star takes a deep breath and I lean in, listening patiently.

"I texted Woody to set up a time to talk. I didn't want to interrupt his day." She wrings her hands in her lap. "But he didn't respond. I tried calling, and I texted again…"

"He probably just needs time to cool off." I don't say that out loud, but it's more likely that Woody's punishing her for walking out.

"That's what I thought," she continues. "Until I tried using my bank card at the market."

Tears start to flow. Mom hands her a tissue and jumps in to fill in the blanks.

"They have a joint bank account over at BRC. Star's card wouldn't work at the store, so she tried logging into the app, and it appears someone changed the password and security questions for the account."

Star looks at me wide-eyed. "I put my savings and my mom's life insurance money into that account."

I start to fume. "That bastard."

"He can't just do that, can he?" Martha looks at me.

"Your name is on the account, right?"

"Yes," Star says. "It's a joint account. I went into the bank with him and showed my ID."

"Then he can't just steal your money. There are laws."

"But his dad is the law." Star's eyes shine with tears.

"The Wades might be able to interfere locally. But this is a bank."

"A local bank," Star says.

She has a good point. I don't know how much actual power Sheriff Wade can exert over Bell River Community Bank, but he can certainly interfere.

"You understand this is an attempt to regain control over you, right?"

Star nods, sinking deeper into the couch. "I guess so."

"And you definitely do not want to go back to Woody?"

"Definitely not." The fire in her eyes tells me she means it.

"Then we'll figure it out. If he wants to make it ugly, you can, too. You can threaten him with a smear campaign."

"Good idea," Martha says. "The last thing that awful man wants is bad press."

"But—" Star's phone rings on the table, surprising us all. She stares at the device as if it might bite.

Martha picks the call up. "Yes?" She hands it to Star. "It's Shane."

"Hi Shane. I'm fine. You can? Okay, I'll see you in an hour." Star looks up, smiling.

"What's that about?" I say, curious.

"Star has some valuable items at the house," Mom explains. "Jewelry and things."

"Shane says he'll help me sell my stuff online. Jenna, can you give me a ride home—I mean to Woody's? It's his poker night. I can pick up everything and get my car while he's out."

On the drive to Woody's, I learn that Star's Chrysler sedan was her grandma Lara's and is fully paid off. She also has a credit card in her own name with some wiggle room, and the code to Woody's gate is his birthday. All good information.

We pass through the giant gate with the W and pull up the driveway. Star veers to the side of the house. Woody's truck is gone, but there's a cherry-red Jeep parked next to Star's car.

"That was fast," she mumbles as she steps onto the pavement.

"Whose Jeep is that?" I ask, warily.

"You'll see." Star leads me through the unlocked mudroom door.

Voices drift in from the living room.

"Have you found a wife yet?" says a man's voice. "Or are you planning on offending every young lady until there are none left? Is Mother aware?"

"Aware of what?" a woman answers back.

I stop Star and whisper. "What's going on?"

Star takes a deep breath, and we step into the living room.

Peyton Honeycutt is lounging on the white couch, wearing a white silk robe, sipping white wine and watching *Bridgerton*. When she sees us, she freezes the picture, and her jaw drops ever so slightly.

"What are you doing here?" Peyton demands.

"I live here," Star crosses her arms. "You?"

"I'm helping a dear friend through a difficult time." Peyton grins and leans back into the couch. "Woody didn't tell me you'd be dropping by."

"Well, Peyton, he didn't tell me he was sleeping with you," Star says. "That's Woody for you. Full of surprises."

For a moment, Peyton Honeycutt seems to be at a loss for her usual array of nasty words. It's nice to see Star standing up for herself.

Then the terror of Bell River High recovers her rancor. "You always were a buzzkill, Star. Like that time at Cheer Camp when you thought everyone should win a prize—"

"Peyton, we're just here to pick up Star's car and some clothes," I say. As much as I enjoy their verbal sparring, we need to get in and out before trouble arrives in the form of Woody.

"Fine." Peyton waves a hand dismissively. "But be fast. I don't want you here when Woody gets home. You've upset him enough already."

Star and I head upstairs and quickly pack two suitcases, filling them with jeans, T-shirts, and sweaters and leaving behind the impressive number of beige suits. Then she grabs her jewelry box, and we lug everything downstairs.

"I'll just be a second," Star says, walking toward Woody's office.

"Where are you going?" Peyton flutters after her down the hall.

"Just a few more things." Star pulls a key out of pocket and slips it in the doorknob.

"You can't go in there." Peyton's voice is shrill. "Nobody is allowed in there without permission."

Star smiles and turns the knob.

"I'm calling Woody," Peyton warns.

"Go right ahead. It's poker night. His phone will be turned off."

Peyton pauses for a moment, then counters with, "Then I'll call his dad."

Star and I exchange a surprised look. Peyton may be smarter than we gave her credit for all these years.

"Listen, Peyton." Star steps back from the door. "There's a box in the back of the office closet. It's full of mementos, some of my mom's things, baby pictures. That's all I want."

"I don't know..." Peyton's expression softens for a split second.

"Please?"

Then her mean girl mask snaps back in place. Peyton knows she has the upper hand.

"Nope," she says. "No way."

I expect Star to crumble. Instead, she surprises me.

"I'll make you a deal, Peyton. Let me get my stuff. You can make sure that's all I take. Then we'll relock this door, and I'll get out of your life forever. You can have Woody all to yourself. Isn't that what you've always wanted?"

"You'll leave him? Officially?" Her eyes light up.

"I promise," Star says.

A sly smile crosses Peyton's lips. "What will I tell him?"

"Nothing," I suggest, encouraging her worst instincts. "Go home. Tell him you had a headache. You left and never saw us."

Peyton narrows her eyes and looks directly at Star. "How can I trust you?"

I almost feel sorry for Peyton that she thinks controlling, manipulative Woody is a catch.

"I'll leave a note. You can watch me write it."

Peyton thinks over the offer. "Okay. Hurry."

Star walks into the office and opens a closet door. Buried deep in the back is a bankers box with *Storage* written on the side. She carries it out and Peyton briefly inspects the contents. As promised, the box is full of odds and ends, photos and knick-knacks. Star hands me the box and locks the office. Then she walks to a white side table, pulls a pen and pad from a drawer, and writes a note in cursive. She holds the paper up for Peyton to inspect.

Woody -
I never want to see you again.
- Star

She leaves the note on the table and tosses the office key to Peyton.

"He's all yours. But if you think life with Woody will be like the story you're watching, you're in for a surprise."

Peyton shrugs, but she doesn't exactly seem confident.

The Chrysler keys are hanging on one of the entryway hooks. By the time we've loaded Star's car, Peyton has changed into her street clothes and is climbing into her Jeep.

The three of us snake down the curved driveway, through the ostentatious gate, and onto the empty street. As I pause to make sure the gate closes, my phone buzzes. I glance down expecting a victory text from Star.

Dylan: *Dinner tomorrow?*

A flush of excitement races through me.

Me: *Sure.*
Dylan: *7pm Boomers. Maybe teach me some of your pool shark tricks after?*
Me: *Sounds great.*
Dylan: *It's a date.*

Chapter 16
Date Night

A light, powdery dusting of snow falls as I walk up the path to Boomer's Bistro. The Christmas fairy lights are still up and sparkling as I pass beneath the green awning and through the door. Even though it's ridiculous for me to consider dating right now, here I am, about to meet Dylan Connor. His text was pretty irresistible.

If I were going to rate my nervousness on a scale from one to ten, I'd say I'm firmly an eight. Checking myself in the entryway mirrors, I pinch some color in my cheeks and smooth my hair to ensure I'm presentable. At Dave's insistence I threw a clingy space-dyed sweater dress with a '70s vibe into my suitcase last minute. Thank goodness I listened to him. I've styled it with knee-high boots and thick leggings. The end result is weather-appropriate but dressed up enough for a dinner date.

Glancing around the restaurant, the mood is festive. The glass is crystal clear, the brass fixtures polished, and buttery candlelight flickers on every table. Cool jazz plays over the speakers, giving the atmosphere a warm, relaxed vibe. An aroma of sugar, butter, and freshly baked pastry wafts from the kitchen. A scattering of people are enjoying their dinner.

Boomer spots me and walks over, wearing a clean, starched apron. He looks me up and down approvingly.

"Well, don't you paint a picture," he says. "Your date is over here."

Boomer leads me around the corner to a quiet alcove where Dylan Connor is waiting. His fitted charcoal suit jacket is open, revealing a black shirt with a subtle texture. The collar is unbuttoned. He's stylish but relaxed. A bottle of Dom Pérignon is on ice. Crystal champagne flutes are waiting to be filled. I feel like I've stepped into a scene from a romance novel.

When he sees me, Dylan stands up and slides my chair in as I sit down. Then he hands me a bouquet of the most breathtaking roses I've ever seen. They're deep violet with tinges of blue, an impossible color. The scent is fresh and intoxicating.

"I had these flown in from a florist in New York," he says as if that's normal.

"They're beautiful," I marvel. "I didn't know such a color existed."

"Japanese scientists found a way to increase the blue pigment." He picks up the bottle of Dom. "May I pour you a glass?"

"That would be lovely." He hands me a flute of pale champagne. Our glasses chime as they touch.

"If the past is a prelude—tonight was worth waiting for." He meets my eyes as we sip.

"Maybe," I say, blushing. The champagne bubbles tickle, and the flavor is light, dry, and delicate. It's like sipping dew drops filled with sunlight. If Dylan is trying to make up for the past, he's off to a good start.

Boomer brings our menus.

"Is there anything you don't eat? I'd love to order for us," Dylan says.

I nod, relaxing. "Go ahead." I've had a couple of rough days, and it feels nice to have someone take the wheel for a change.

"Let's see." Dylan's eyes light up as he scans the menu. "I see you have some new dishes, Boomer. How are the scallops with pomegranate and Meyer lemon?"

"Delicious, if I do say so." Boomer's smile could light up the whole town of Bell River.

"Then let's start with those, followed by duck deux façons with green peppercorn sauce. Promise me you'll never take that one off the menu."

"No chance. The duck is Cece's favorite."

"Thank goodness for Cece." Dylan smiles, and hands Boomer back the menu. "Surprise us for dessert?"

"My pleasure." Boomer tops off our champagne and disappears.

"So, I finally get you alone." Dylan smiles. "You've changed, you know."

"Have I?" Suddenly, I feel self-conscious.

"You seem more…confident. It suits you."

"I suppose we're both different." I tuck a creamy white napkin in my lap.

"How's Star doing?" There's concern in Dylan's eyes.

"Getting stronger every day."

"I feel so stupid. We all know Woody can be a jerk, but I had no idea he was hurting her. I feel, I don't know, responsible in some way." He seems genuinely upset.

"Woody had good reason to watch his behavior around you. Your dad contributes to his campaign."

"Not anymore. At least not if I can help it," he says. "And I was thinking, we have some vacant property in town. I'm going to talk to my dad about letting Star stay in one of our places until she's on her feet."

"That would be amazing, Dylan." I'm genuinely impressed. Could he be any more charming?

Boomer delivers our first course and it's delicious. The scallops are perfectly caramelized on the outside. Sweet and tender inside, and resting on a bright, tangy sauce.

Dylan and I fall into comfortable conversation. He makes me laugh, bringing up silly memories and crazy things that happened at the Winter Festival. He talks about the characters he encounters managing his family's properties. The reason I fell for Dylan in the first place comes rushing back. He's sweet, self-effacing and funny.

As soon as our forks touch the empty plates, a server sweeps them away, and the main dish arrives. As light and delicate as our first course was, the duck is rich, gamey, and piquant.

If you had told me I'd be enjoying a fantastic meal at a lovely bistro in Bell River with Dylan Connor, I never would have believed it.

Finally, we face each other across a single plate of French cream puffs filled with Dolce De Leche ice cream and drizzled with dark chocolate. We take turns scooping up the luscious dessert.

"So, how's your internship going?" Dylan politely steers the conversation to me.

"Better than I expected. Detective Myers is brilliant, and Maggie is so amazing." Maybe it's the champagne, but I find myself opening up. "The best part is, there are some new developments in my brother's case."

"Really?" Dylan says. "That's great. Nothing dangerous, I hope?"

"Nothing I can't handle." I leave it at that. No need to scare him off with stories of my past run-ins with Stockade Wade and mysterious SUVS.

He smiles. "After that pool game, I have a feeling you can handle anything."

"I hope so." A warm feeling washes over me. He's so supportive.

"Promise you'll call if I can help with Tyler's case?" Dylan asks.

"Definitely." I spoon a bite of ice cream in my mouth.

Boomer arrives at our table. "How was everything?"

"Incredible," Dylan says.

"*Merci beaucoup.*" Boomer sets down the check and disappears.

"It's still early." Dylan looks at me with searing dark eyes. "Want to get a nightcap?"

I feel myself blush. "Well—"

A loud sound, like nails on a chalkboard, interrupts my answer. A dark-haired man in a worn leather jacket and black jeans is dragging a heavy chair to our table—Cole Braedon? What the hell?

"Well, this is cozy," Cole says. "Are those Suntory Roses? Nice touch." He reaches over, plucks one of the roses out of the bouquet, snaps the stem, and sticks the violet flower through a buttonhole on his jacket. "I think I would have gone with Juliets myself. More dramatic. Less showy."

"Who the hell are you? What do you want?" Dylan demands, eyes flashing with irritation.

Cole tilts his head curiously, green eyes focused on Dylan. Then he smirks. "I'm here to talk to Jenna. You don't mind, do you?"

"Seriously? Can't we talk later?" I haven't seen Cole Braedon since our paths crossed on a case last fall. What's he doing here— in Bell River—on my date?

"I'm confused," Dylan says, tight-lipped. "You know this guy?"

"Of course, she knows me." Cole picks up my champagne flute and drinks from the glass.

"Well, I—" How do I begin to explain?

"I don't get it," Dylan says. "Is he your boyfriend?"

"Definitely not. More like a colleague," I say flatly. "And I'm just as surprised as you are. Dylan, meet Cole."

"Oh, come on, Jenna. You're hurting my feelings," Cole says, pointing to the silver Claddagh on my finger. "You are wearing my ring, after all." He grins broadly.

"Is that true?" Dylan says, baffled. "Did he give you that ring?"

A flash of frustration surges through me, followed by embarrassment. "It's complicated," I manage to say, wishing I could crawl under the table. On a scale of first-date catastrophes, this has got to be a ten.

Dylan stands up, throws his napkin on the table, and buttons his jacket.

"I have no idea what's going on here, but I don't have time for this," he scowls. "I'll call you later, Jenna. Maybe you can explain what's going on without your colleague around."

"Dylan, I—" But he's already gone. He and Boomer confer as he handles the bill before pulling on his overcoat and disappearing out the front door.

"Touchy," Cole says, eyeing the remaining dessert. "Are you going to eat that?"

Cole takes a last bite of cream puff and sets down his spoon. Boomer walks over to the table and tilts his head curiously, locking eyes with my new guest.

"Is everything alright, Jenna?" Boomer asks. "I see Mr. Connor left early."

"Um, I think he had an appointment," I lie, resigned to the fact my date is hopelessly ruined.

Cole Braedon has a terrible habit of interfering with my life. Sometimes I think he enjoys screwing with me. But it's hard to stay mad at him. Cole's done more for me and Tyler than I could ever repay.

"Can I get you anything else?" Boomer says, motioning to the busboy, who begins clearing the table.

"Les choux à la crème étaient délicieux," Cole says in perfect French.

Wait. Cole speaks French? Of course, he does.

"Merci, êtes-vous français?" Boomer replies, surprised.

"J'ai passé du temps à Paris." Cole shrugs. They chat back and forth in French. Within a few minutes, Boomer is laughing. I don't speak the language, but Dave went to Paris earlier this year, and ever since, he's been practicing on an app that teaches you via French TV. So I understand only "un petit" amount of the conversation. They're reminiscing about the good old days in Paris.

Finally, Cole says, "Dis-moi, tu as un bon cognac?"

"J'ai juste la chose." Boomer smiles and disappears, returning with a bottle, two brandy glasses, and a dish of chocolate-covered strawberries. He holds up the amber bottle labeled Frapin XO. The candlelight flickers, making the gold letters sparkle.

Cole breaks into a huge smile. "Ah, you're in for a treat, Jenna. One of the oldest vineyards in France, dating to the thirteenth century."

Boomer pours the cognac. I take a sip. Oh, my Lord. It tastes like a fiery drop of the sun—complex, smooth, and delicious. No wonder people drink brandy.

"Notes of caramel, chocolate, and dried fruit," Cole says. "Vivre la vie au maximum."

"Live life to the fullest?" I translate. I happen to know that one.

"Vous êtes un homme sage," Boomer says and disappears.

Cole sets his glass down and fixes his deep green eyes on mine.

"So, a date, huh?" he asks. "What do you see in that guy?"

"None of your business," I huff, caught between our undeniable chemistry and my anger with him for intruding.

"Trust fund baby." Cole shakes his head. "Lucky I'm here to stop you from making a terrible mistake."

"What mistake?" Suddenly I have an urge to drink the entire glass of cognac. Cole Braedon, or some 13th-century version of him, is why cognac was probably invented.

"Tsk, tsk. You don't want to get involved with a guy with a record, do you?"

"No way Dylan Connor has a record."

"Maybe not now. But it can be arranged." He hands me a chocolate-covered strawberry.

My God, he's infuriating. "Why are you here anyway?"

"I was doing work for the FBI and Interpol in Albany."

"What work is that?"

"Investigating the Happy Kat drug ring."

I stop mid-strawberry. "Are you serious? Interpol is involved?"

"Technically, that's classified. But imagine my surprise when Detective Cece Myers arrested brothers Stanley and Jayson Spar for possessing HK—assisted by one Jenna Stack."

"But the whole thing was dropped," I stammer. "How did you find out?"

"Anything you say on the TAC channel is recorded. I had a regular search going for certain types of incidents. Detective Myers radioed a fellow officer to report she had a sample of Happy Kat.

The next thing I know, the case disappears. Do you have any idea what happened?"

"We arrested the Spar brothers and started to book them. Then, Sheriff Wade destroyed the evidence. They're his nephews."

I get the rare satisfaction of seeing a surprised look on Cole's face.

"You mean Stockade Wade? The same guy who arrested your brother?" Cole leans back in his chair and whistles. "Okay, now we're getting somewhere. That man has a bad reputation. Corruption, bribes."

"So, you think Wade could be involved with the Happy Kat ring somehow?"

"Maybe. His nephews certainly are. The drugs always hit the street at the same time, and the territory is expanding. A shipment was just busted in Belgium."

I try to control my excitement. I need to find out what Cole knows. Direct questions won't work. Maybe I can give him another piece of information.

"Listen, Cole, there's something else." I hand him my phone and press play. The man on tape from the Super Sports plays.

"What am I looking at?" Cole says, intrigued.

"CCTV footage of a potential suspect in the Vitner murder."

"Good work," Cole says. "What about a paper trail? Did you locate any receipts?"

"The store burned down before we could look through them. Arson."

"That can't be a coincidence. You need to be careful, Jenna." Cole frowns. "I mean it."

"I will." Even though I answer casually, we both know I won't stop until I find the real killer.

For a moment, he seems thrown off, lost in thought. Then he

reaches into his jacket and pulls out a black box. "I almost forgot. This is for you."

A gift? Cole is so weird, and his timing is the worst. But I have to admit, I'm excited to open it. Inside the box is an elegant pocketknife with a curved, inlaid handle. I hold it in my hand. The balance is perfect. I open and close the blade smoothly with a solid lock. What is it about the men in my life giving me weapons? First, Serge bought me a gun. Now Cole gives me a knife. Do I seem hostile or something?

"It's a William Henry," he says.

"It's beautiful." I admire the workmanship, turning the blade.

Cole seems pleased with himself as he pays for the cognac and says goodbye to his new friend.

"Are you coming?" He stands up and zips his jacket.

"Where?"

"It's time we talked with the Spar brothers."

Chapter 17
Hater

The Spar brothers' street is a dozen blocks from Cece's but looks eerily similar, a smattering of well-maintained homes sprinkled among run-down and empty properties. The biggest difference is that most of the streetlights are out and there's a wall covered in graffiti. On one corner is a half-melted snowman. A skinny orange cat darts across the road and slips under a splintered fence.

Cole parks and turns off the lights. Across the road is a gray house with a sagging porch. A brand-new lime green Dodge Challenger sits in the driveway. The front picture window is wide enough to see two figures sitting in front of a big-screen TV, playing a violent video game.

"Come on," Cole says and opens the driver's side door.

"You mean we're just going to walk up there?"

"Why not? We're only here for a friendly conversation."

We approach the house. Cole rings the bell. Through the window, Jay and Stan have a brief exchange that can be easily translated—they decide not to answer the door.

Cole rings again, then shoves his hands in his pockets whistling.

The Spars ignore us and keep playing.

"Wait here. If either of them comes through this door, stop them."

"Stop them? How am I supposed to do that?"

"Instinct. You learn hand signals yet?"

"Kind of."

Cole grins and walks past the picture window to a smaller one at the side of the house, closer to where they are playing. He raps loudly on the glass with his FBI credentials.

"FBI, we need a word…"

Jay and Stan glance over and panic. Jay bolts toward the back of the house, and Stan heads my way. Cole flashes me the hand signs for carry out your assigned task.

I have a split second to decide my strategy. Tripping him leaves too much room for error. There's nothing on the porch to swing at him. So I position myself at the side of the door frame, and as soon as the door swings opens, I drive my elbow into Stan's sternum and knock the wind out of him.

Stan staggers back into the entryway, shocked, video game controller still in his hand. He doubles over trying to catch his breath, so I grab his shoulders.

"Listen, Stan, we just want to talk."

Cole walks up with Jay in tow. "Nice job, Stack."

"What the hell?" Jay sputters. "This is our place, man."

"I rang." Cole shrugs. "You ran."

"W-what do you want?" Unlike his brother, Stan seems scared.

"Just a few questions," I answer calmly. "That's all. Can we all just sit down?"

Jay looks back and forth between us. "Fine," he scowls. "But we got nothin' to say."

The living room is littered with beer cans, fast food wrappers, and brand new, name-brand trainers. The furniture is garish but sturdy and looks new. A stack of unopened boxes leans in the corner, presumably full of more purchases. Jay and Stan take a seat on the couch. Cole and I clear off a pair of red velvet club chairs and sit down.

"Who is this guy?" Jay keeps up the attitude, but his brow is wrinkled with worry lines.

Cole raises a hand to stop me from replying.

"My name isn't important." He leans forward. "What is important is who I represent. Federal. International. Big boy crime fighters. The kind that eat up boys like you—and your uncle—for lunch and then laugh about it. Do you understand me?"

Jay crosses his arms defiantly. Stan looks at the floor.

"I'll take that as a yes. I'm sure you've seen the TV shows. We know losers like you will never change. You'll get incarcerated, killed, or both before too long. We're happy to help you get there. But we mostly care about the bosses. So, I'm going to tell you what I know. Okay?"

Cole is magnificent. He's both good cop and bad cop, reasonable and terrifying. A master of manipulation and control, he waits patiently for an answer while the brothers squirm in uncomfortable silence.

Jay finally growls, "You don't know shit."

"I know there's no way your YouTube channel income is covering your lifestyle. And that's not just supposition. We've done the math." Cole leans back and drums his fingers on the red velvet armrest. "I also know a high school kid in Albany overdosed on Happy Kat. Not only does a witness place you in the area at the time, the lab guys can match seized drugs—like from a dead kid's bedroom—to a dealer's supply. You don't know it yet, but the heat is breathing down on your entire operation.

We'll have warrants soon. Your days are numbered, boys." Cole sighs as if he feels sorry for them. "So, if you don't give me something I can use before I walk out that door, things are going to get ugly."

"It's not our operation," Stan blurts.

"Exactly. So why go down for it?" Cole glances toward the kitchen. "You got any beer? I can use a beer. Anyone else?"

The Spars seem stunned by the change of topic. I suppress a smile and shake my head.

"No? Okay," He shrugs and points at Jay. "I'll be right back. If you run. I'll shoot you for resisting arrest."

As he leaves the room, Cole winks and touches his nose. That's the hand signal for a big, fat lie. He's enjoying himself.

"Is this guy for real?" Jay says.

I lean back in my chair. "Oh, he's real alright. Special ops kind of real. And he means what he says. I recommend cooperating."

"Fuck this. Come on, bro." Jay stands up.

Stan looks even more nervous. "I don't want go down for—"

"Shut up!" Jay warns.

Cole enters the room with a can of beer in one hand and his gun in the other. "You've got two choices. Twenty years in prison when this whole thing blows open, or one short, confidential conversation with us now."

"You can keep us out of jail?" Stan asks, wide-eyed.

"I can't guarantee *no* time, but I have influence, and I always help my friends. Just ask Jenna."

"That's true," I say. "He can be very helpful."

"And I'm a much better friend than enemy. Why don't you two confer."

Cole holsters his gun, sits back down, and opens his beer. So far, the fact he's drinking beer is the most surprising thing to me.

We wait in silence as the Spars whisper back and forth. Stan looks positively ill, and Jay has caught his paranoia. Finally, they face Cole.

"Okay," Stan announces. "Deal."

"But you better not screw us over," Jay adds.

Cole dives right in with the obvious question, "Where are you getting the drugs?"

"From a P.O. box," Stan says.

"Go on." Cole drinks his beer. "Walk me through the process."

"We have a key. We pick up a manila envelope with the product inside. We leave an envelope with the money. That's it."

"You don't know who picks the money up?"

Stan shrugs. "Nope."

"What about the drugs? Who's your supplier?"

"No idea," Jay says. "Even our first contact was anonymous."

"They slipped a letter under the front door," Stan says.

"Aren't you curious?" Cole presses.

"Hell no. The less we know, the better," Jay says.

"Until you're trading information for leniency," I point out. "Is it just Happy Kat? I know you sold steroids in high school."

Cole pulls out a pack of cigarettes and offers them a smoke. "Tell her anything she wants to know, exactly like you're talking to me."

Jay accepts one of Cole's strong, black cigarettes before answering. "We sold steroids back in high school. But not anymore."

My pulse quickens. "Where did you get the steroids?"

Jay takes a drag of the cigarette, his face turns red, and he immediately starts coughing.

I look at Stan, who answers for his gasping brother, "Same supplier. Same drill. The product has changed, but not the system. First, it was pot, then steroids, a little oxy, and now it's Happy Kat. We're just soldiers. Someone else decides what the people want."

"Not soldiers," I correct him. "Pushers. And that's a felony."

I'm disappointed not to get a name, but Cole's case and Tyler's overlap, so I feel encouraged.

"What if you need a supply change? Who do you contact?" Cole says.

"We don't." Stan says. "We just leave a note for next time."

"When's the next pickup?"

"This weekend," Stan says as Jay continues to cough.

Cole takes a last swig of beer, drops his cigarette in the empty can, and stands up.

"That's it?" Jay has recovered enough to rejoin the conversation.

"Yep. Business as usual." Cole gives them a hard look. "Don't tell anyone about this conversation. Understand?"

"We get it, man." Stan's voice is hopeful. "And you'll look out for us?"

"Keep your mouth shut, and I'll do what I can. Blab, and I'll make it my personal mission to destroy your lives."

Cole brushes past them, and I follow.

"Well, that was fun," I say as we climb into his car.

Cole laughs. "For us, maybe."

The Spars stand in the window watching as Cole uses their driveway to turn around. I buckle my seat belt for the short ride home.

"I'm leaving town for a few days, but I'll be back. Wanna join me for a stakeout?"

"Definitely."

"It's a date." He smiles. "Now don't double book with some idiot."

We ride in comfortable silence the rest of the way until Cole pulls up in front of Martha's place. A curtain cracks open as nosy Annie Dupont spies from the second floor.

"I'm glad you have a snooping neighbor," Cole says and turns toward me. "You were great back there." He leans in closer. "But—"

"What?"

"Listen, Jenna," Cole hits a switch to unlock the door. "Don't discuss this new intel with anyone, not even someone you trust. You could accidentally slip information. Understood?"

"I get it. We don't know who's involved."

"That includes that nosy neighbor up there. So, I'm going to walk you to the door. And you're going to kiss me."

"I'm going to what?"

"You heard me. It's better if she thinks this was just a date."

Cole gets out of the car and opens my door. We walk up the steps together and just before we reach the door, he looks at me with his stormy green eyes and slips his arm around my waist. Then he pulls me close and kisses me. His lips are soft and probing. As he draws me closer, the heat rises between us, and I pull away slightly to catch my breath.

"Okay, I just—"

"Make it look good, Jenna."

This time when he kisses me, it's deep and passionate. For a moment, my head spins before he releases me.

"Best part of the job." He smiles. "See you this weekend."

Above me I hear a window rattle and Annie Dupont's voice. "Well, I never."

My heart is beating as I cross the threshold and lean my back against the wall to catch my breath. The scene has vastly improved over last night. Mom and Star are curled up in the living room, playing cards and laughing. Alex and Eliza are dozing together in a basket on the floor. A picked-over plate of homemade chocolate chip cookies and an empty wine bottle tell me they've been at it for a while.

"Finally!" Star tosses her cards on the table. "How was it?"

My stomach tightens. With everything that's happened tonight —Cole showing up, grilling the Spar brothers, that fake kiss that felt so real—I almost forgot my disastrous date with Dylan.

"Sadly, not great." I set my bag down and unzip my boots.

"Was he a jerk?" Star says.

"No, actually, he was terrific."

"So, what happened?" Mom pats the empty spot on the couch.

I grab a chocolate chip cookie and plop down next to her.

"We ran into a colleague of mine, and things got a little... weird." I try to formulate how to explain Cole's appearance without bringing up the Spars when there's a loud knock on the door.

We freeze and look at each other. Late-night visits are rarely good news.

"Are you expecting someone, honey?" Martha says.

Bang. Bang. Bang. Louder this time.

"Star, I know you're in there. I saw your car out front." Of course, it's Woody Wade.

"I'll handle it." I walk to the front door, reach into my bag and slip the knife Cole gave me into the palm of my hand. Then I look through the peephole. Woody is standing on the porch.

I crack open the door. "Woody, it's late—"

Woody slams his full weight against the door and pushes past me into the room. Alex yowls and both cats dart upstairs.

"Damn you!" He points at Star. "Where's my stuff?

Star recoils on the couch like a cornered animal. "What stuff?"

"You broke into my office and stole my property."

"Calm down, Woody," I say, feeling the weight of the knife in my palm.

"I just took a box of my grandma's stuff," Star says. "Some pictures."

Woody starts tearing around the room, yanking open drawers and cabinets, tossing the contents onto the floor. He kicks a trash can by Martha's desk and papers scatter.

"I put goddamned valuables in that box," Woody huffs. "I need it now."

Why does Woody want that box so much? We need to find out. I give Star a warning look, slowly shaking my head. She nods and sits up straight on the couch.

"It's not here," Star lies. "Please go. Anything that belongs to you, I'll return later."

Woody looks like he's going to blow his top. His face turns bright red. He grabs a corner table and topples it over. "I want my stuff now. Where is it?"

Martha stands up. "Woodrow Wade, I will not have this behavior in my house."

For a moment Woody freezes, staring at my mom. I step in front of Star.

"Let's make a deal, Woody," I say calmly. "When you return Star's money, she'll give you back the box."

Woody growls like an animal and lunges at Star. I push her out of the way. He looks at me, seething with anger.

I brandish the knife. "I'm warning you!"

But Woody's too far gone to hear me. He is the embodiment of rage.

He crouches down, about to rush me, knife or no knife, when Martha grabs the empty wine bottle and hits Woody hard across the side of the head. There's a sickening thud, but it's nothing like you see in the movies. The bottle doesn't break, and Woody doesn't collapse. Instead, he stumbles back, holding his head where a giant lump will no doubt appear.

"You!" he says, turning to Martha. "I'll kill you."

"Everyone freeze!" Cece Myers is standing in the doorway. She has her gun drawn and is pointing it directly at Woody. "Your neighbor called in a disturbance. What's happening here?"

Thank you, nosy Annie.

Woody points at Star. "She stole from me."

"Then you can come down to the station and file a formal complaint," Cece says.

At the words, Woody appears to deflate.

"She has my stuff," Woody whines.

"Mr. Wade, do you want to press charges?"

He considers for a minute. "No, that won't be necessary, as long as—"

"Good decision," Cece cuts him off. She looks around the room at the toppled furniture and paper strewn across the floor.

"Mrs. Stack, do you want to press charges?"

"No, I understand breakups are hard," Martha says tightly.

Anger flashes across Woody's face, but he controls himself.

"What do you say you head home now, Mr. Wade?" Cece suggests. "It's late."

"I think I will. Peyton will be worried." He turns around at the door. "You better find my—"

"If you threaten Miss Simonsen, I will take you to the station myself," Cece says.

Woody slams the door on the way out. After watching him leave, Cece holsters her gun and turns to Star. "That man is dangerous. Get a lawyer and a restraining order. Jenna has my cell number. Anything happens, call me directly."

As soon as Cece is gone, I bolt the door.

The three of us look at each other. We're all thinking the same thing.

"Maybe we should check that box," I say.

Star goes upstairs and retrieves the box. She sets it on top of the kitchen table, and we all look at it curiously. I grab a notepad from the drawer.

"Star? Can you pull out and describe each item while I document the contents."

Martha pulls up a chair to watch. "That sounds very professional, dear."

"One plastic baggie with some costume jewelry. A first edition hardcover of *The Hitchhiker's Guide to the Galaxy*. Shane said this could be worth something if it's in good shape. One set of silver pens. My baby book. A photo album."

"Oh, let me see that, dear. Is it alright to touch the evidence?"

"Go ahead." I scribble to catch up. "All your stuff so far?"

"Yep." She pulls out the photo album, and there's a small shoebox underneath. "Except this." Star opens the smaller box and pushes the contents around. "There's a Bell River High enamel pin, a keychain shaped like a football, and a bunch of photographs."

"Remember that camera he used to carry around?" My mind flashes to an image of seventeen-year-old Woody with an old analog camera around his neck. There were darkrooms at school for the photography course.

"Yeah." Star smiles. "Weird hobby for a jock." She spreads the photos on the table and points. "See? There are photos of Abby, their mom, the football team…"

"If that's all he wanted, why didn't he just say so?" Martha says.

"I don't know," Star says. "But now I feel bad. I should get this back to him."

I look at the pictures, all from Woody's past. They seem important somehow.

"Actually, I think you should hold onto it for now," I say. "It's leverage."

"Okay." Star puts the pictures carefully back. "I'll put the box back under the bed."

"Well, mystery solved," Martha says. "I'm going to sleep. You girls should too. You have a big day tomorrow. Going to Eastmoor is quite a trip."

"Are you sure you don't mind?" Star says to Martha.

"You visiting Tyler in my place? Of course, not. I'm sure he'd love to see you, and I have a full schedule of tutoring." Martha starts up the stairs. "Don't mind the mess, I'll clean up tomorrow."

"Mom?"

"Yes?"

"That was a nice right hook."

"Thank you, dear."

Chapter 18
Eastmoor Correctional Facility

The Eastmoor Correctional Facility is intimidating. The few windows that can be seen are covered in metal bars. The building itself is in disrepair, with water stains on the ceiling, the smell of mold, and cracks along the walls. I can sense Star's dread as we move through the series of bag searches, ID checks, and metal detectors to enter the facility.

"Poor Tyler," Star whispers. "This place is awful."

"It's kind of rough, but he has protection," I remind her. Thanks to a mob lawyer I know called Manny the Rock, conditions have improved for my baby brother.

After waiting for what seems like an eternity, Star and I are allowed into the large visiting room. There are about a dozen other people, mostly women and kids, waiting for prisoners to arrive. The walls are a beige putty color, and the mismatched institutional furniture is bolted to the floor. Star fidgets nervously in a stiff plastic chair. I've done this enough to know we could be waiting here a while, so I try to distract her.

"When was the last time you saw Ty?"

She bites her lip, thinking. "I guess it was the trial?"

"I know he appreciated you being there. We all did."

For a moment, we're both quiet. The trial is a bad memory for anyone who cares for Tyler. The prosecution was relentless, and the defense was hobbled by an unsympathetic judge.

"I feel awful," Star whispers. "I should have visited—"

"Don't feel bad. Just understand...Tyler's not a kid anymore. He's changed in these past four years. He's not the same as you remember."

There's a loud clanging noise as the heavy electronic door unlocks and slides open.

A guard escorts an Eastmoor inmate into the visiting room. He's uncuffed to join his family, and the joy they feel is palpable as they embrace.

Star smiles. "Remember how we used to take Ty ice skating?" she says wistfully. "How old was he then?"

"We were maybe sixteen? I think he was around eleven."

"Wow." Her eyes go wide. "We were the same age he was when...it happened."

The "it" she's referring to is Tyler's arrest for Coach Vitner's murder.

The heavy door opens again. This time Tyler steps in wearing handcuffs, escorted by a stern-faced guard. He turns and holds up his hands. The guard uncuffs him. His dark green jumpsuit is rolled up at the sleeves, exposing strong muscles and an assortment of prison tattoos. He walks over, and we hug briefly. The guard watches every move and nods.

Tyler slips into a chair and leans back.

"Hey J...Hey Star," he says, with a measured demeanor.

Judging by the way his hazel eyes light up, seeing Star is a nice surprise.

"You look so...different," Star says, a little startled. "You're all grown up."

"Must be the weightlifting." Tyler shrugs. My brother's change is more than skin-deep. He carries himself with the kind of self-possession that comes from meeting challenges and overcoming them. I only hope the obstacles he's had to work through don't scar him for life.

"How's Manny?" I say.

"Great. He's king of this place." Tyler laughs. Then he turns to Star. "By the way, thanks for writing. I love your letters."

Star blushes and looks away. "I'm just sorry I haven't—"

"Don't be," he interrupts her. "I realize this place is tough. How's Woody?"

"We broke up." She smiles as if dumping Woody is an accomplishment.

"Good." He grins mischievously. "He was always a dick."

I shake my head at his insensitivity. "Come on, Ty."

"It's okay, Ty's right," Star says. "Woody is abusive, and I'm happy to be rid of him."

Our universal agreement that Woody is a jerk puts everyone at ease. Star's shoulders relax, and Tyler's mood is less defensive. They smile at each other, and I swear I catch a flush in Tyler's cheeks. Are they flirting? Growing up, he always had a crush on Star. Now that they're both in their twenties, a relationship isn't so far-fetched. But as sweet as their chemistry is, we only have a limited amount of time to talk.

"Listen, Ty—there's a suspect in Coach Vitner's murder."

"Really? Who?" Tyler says, growing serious.

"We don't know his identity yet. But he went to the Super Sports the same day Coach was murdered and bought a ski mask, hooded sweatshirt, and trainers."

"You're kidding me!" Tyler says.

"I'm getting close to finding answers."

"But you need to ask some questions?" Tyler says. "Shoot."

"So the night of the murder, you were at Coach Vitner's house, talking about the fact some of your teammates were on steroids?"

"Right. I saw them shooting up under the bleachers."

"And Coach asked if you knew where they were getting the drugs?"

"Yes. And I told him I didn't know about steroids, but the rumor was the Spars got weed from some guy in Albany. They used to sell behind McCabe's. I felt bad telling him, but that stuff is messed up."

"You did the right thing." Star touches his hand to reassure him. The electricity between them sizzles.

"But weed isn't steroids," I say. "So how did Coach react when you mentioned the Spars?"

Tyler leans back and thinks for a moment.

"He said he already suspected the Spars and that they were just the middlemen. That the guy importing the steroids was the real monster."

"Did it seem like Coach knew who that was?"

"I remember we were in the kitchen. Mrs. Vitner wasn't home, but she'd made lemon squares." Tyler gets a little choked up. "And Coach said, 'Watch out, kid. People aren't always what they seem.'"

"Oh Ty, I'm so sorry," Star says. This time, Tyler reaches out to her, and they hold hands.

"That's all I know, J."

"Okay." I stand up. "I'm going to get us drinks from the vending machine."

I walk over to the dingy old machine and pop quarters in the slots. I take my time, watching the body language of Tyler and Star. I guess the letters these two have been exchanging run a bit deeper than I knew. Tyler leans in toward her, keeping the prescribed distance but meeting her eyes with what looks like longing. She responds by squeezing his hand and looking down shyly. I never thought about Tyler and Star together, but now that I see them, they're perfect. Both are compassionate and thoughtful, and they've both been through a lot. As I walk back and give them their drinks, I overhear the end of the conversation.

"I wish there was something I could do," Star says.

"Could you visit me once in a while?" Tyler says. "I'd really love that."

Star smiles at him. "I will. I promise."

"Time," the guard announces. Star and Tyler reluctantly release each other's hands. But as he walks away, his smile is so bright, it's as if the sun has emerged from behind a cloud.

I arrive at Bell River police station early but exhausted. The sofa at Martha's isn't terrible, but the trip to Eastmoor was draining. There's always an emotional aftermath to visiting Tyler—guilt, sadness, anger, depression—a cocktail of relentless anxiety that makes me toss and turn all night.

After pouring myself a cup of coffee, I head for the vault. Maggie is already perched on top of the desk, laptop open, files and folders arrayed around her with stickies on various items. The room looks and smells much better than it did when we started. The neatly repacked boxes now outnumber the mildewed, damaged ones.

Maggie looks up from the laptop. "You're early. How'd it go with your brother?"

"He's in good spirits.... considering." I hand her a foil-wrapped slice of Mom's homemade banana bread. "I thought I'd make up for taking yesterday off."

"Ooh, thanks." She unwraps the foil, tears off a corner, and pops it in her mouth. "Did you tell Tyler what's been going on?"

"Yes. We went over the conversation he had with Vitner the night of the murder." I take a seat and kick my feet up on the edge of the desk. "Coach told him the Spars were just the middlemen. That the guy importing the steroids was the real monster."

"That's all in the court record," Maggie says.

"True, but then he said something new that struck me as odd."

"Yeah? What exactly?"

"Apparently, Vitner said, 'Watch out, kid. People aren't always what they seem.'"

"Hmmm." Maggie's brow furrows. "That's funny—as if he suspected somebody."

"That's what I thought." I sip my coffee and mull over the clues. "So far, we have the suppressed hair evidence, and a mysterious man at Super Sports buying what looks like the prowler outfit used the night of the murder. Our only lead to hard evidence was receipts that burned up in a fire. Then a weird SUV tries to run me off the road—"

"What? An SUV tried to run you down?" Maggie says, surprised.

I shrug. "Maybe…I'm just counting clues right now."

"Okay, go on."

"The fact that the Spar brothers have no idea where the drugs they sell come from—"

"Wait! You talked to the Spar brothers?" Maggie is struggling to keep up.

"Long story, but yes. I asked them a few questions. They receive drug shipments anonymously." Cole can forget about his "don't discuss the case" rule. I need someone to talk this through with, and he's not around.

Maggie nods, accepting my explanation without question. "Sounds like Coach Vitner may have known the supplier..." She picks at her banana bread like a delicate bird.

"So, the source might have lived in town." I finish her thought. "Maybe the supplier thought Vitner was onto him, so he killed him?"

"Sounds plausible."

"It's so frustrating," I say, finishing my coffee. "We still have no clue who the real murderer is. The case is at an impasse."

Maggie carefully spreads out her empty aluminum foil on the desk and begins to fold the edges into precise sections. "Have you ever heard of Complexity Theory?" She points to one of her books. The spine looks crazy, with geometric figures at odd angles.

"No, what is it? And give me the 'For Dummies' version, please."

Maggie continues to fold and crease the foil.

"It's the study of complex and chaotic systems. What appears to be chaos can eventually yield order, pattern, and structure. Right now, we have a number of what seem to be independent pieces of data or clues to the murder. It's chaotic, so it doesn't make sense. But according to Complexity Theory, if you keep digging, the data will rearrange itself into a coherent system."

She places a perfect origami bird on the desk.

"Dear God, all those books you've been reading have created a monster."

Officer Pete appears in the doorway with a solemn expression.

"There's been a break-in at The Curiosities & Comics Emporium," Pete says. "Cece wants you with her, Jenna. She's waiting out front."

"Shane?" Maggie's cheeks drain of color. She looks stricken.

"Don't panic." Pete says, holding his hand up. "Shane's fine. He's the one who called it in. Looks like it happened overnight."

Maggie picks up her phone and starts texting frantically.

"Don't worry, Magpie, I'll make sure he's safe."

I grab my stuff and head for Cece's squad car.

The front door of The Curiosities & Comics Emporium has obviously been picked. There are telltale scratches around the keyways on both the deadbolt and doorknob. Cece hands me a pair of latex gloves. I pull them on and follow her inside.

The familiar *Star Trek* door chime greets us, but the shop is unrecognizable. Bookshelves are toppled, spinning racks over-turned, and display cases smashed. The floor is covered with piles of ripped and damaged comics, broken glass, and splintered wood. Monster models and action figures with torn limbs are scattered among vintage electronics, rare books, and open board games, their pieces scattered across the floor.

"I'm in here," Shane calls weakly.

The office is just as badly trashed. Every drawer is open and emptied. Bankers boxes full of inventory are dumped out. The LEGO Millennium Falcon Shane put together himself is cracked to pieces as if someone threw it against the wall. Shane sits on the floor, among the debris. He seems like he's in shock.

"Are you okay?" I rush over to him.

"I'm fine. They just trashed my world, is all," he says in despair.

Cece opens her notebook. "Mister Cross, can you tell us what happened?"

Shane looks up at her, takes off his horn-rimmed glasses, and pinches the bridge of his nose.

"I came in at my usual time. The door was open. I found the place like this."

"No burglar alarm?"

He shakes his head.

"Can you tell what's missing?" I steady his arm as he rises to his feet.

"I have to do a complete inventory, but my computer is gone, and they wrecked a lot of stuff..." He walks out to the main shop. "But it's weird..."

Cece and I exchange a glance. Right now, Shane is the one who can see the details we can't, so everything he notices is important.

"What's weird?" Cece prompts him.

Shane points to a pristine comic in a plastic sleeve tossed on the floor. "That's a mint-condition *Tales From The Crypt* #21 from 1950. And over there," Shane points to an untouched display case, "that's a complete set of signed Power Rangers action figures. Super-rare."

"You'll have to excuse me, Mister—"

"Call me Shane."

"Shane, I don't know much about this kind of...stuff. Are those valuable?" Cece says.

"The comic book alone is worth thousands." He runs his hand through his mop of curly hair. "And the action figures are worth bank."

"So why break into a comic shop and leave the best stuff?" Cece says.

The destruction is excessive for a burglary. The upturned boxes draw my attention. A tingling sensation creeps along my spine. Those boxes are identical to the one Star took from Woody's office.

"Maybe they were searching for something else?" I suggest.

"That's what I'm thinking," Cece agrees.

"What about Woody? Maybe he guessed Shane was helping

Star sell her first edition *The Hitchhiker's Guide to the Galaxy*? Was he was looking for that stupid box?"

"Risky behavior for a political candidate," Cece says skeptically. "What about the safe? Didn't you two lock up the CCTV footage?"

"That's right..." I say with a sinking feeling. I was so distracted by the destruction I forgot about the most important thing.

"I checked that first," Shane grins, recovering a little. "Whoever broke in missed it."

Shane leads us to a utility closet adjacent to his office. The door is open, and some cleaning supplies are tipped over. Shane opens an electrical panel. On the surface, it looks normal with breakers and wires. But Shane grabs the edge, pushes down, and the panel snaps free. He removes the fake electronics to reveal a wall safe.

"That's clever," I say as Shane spins the dial.

"The previous tenant put it in. The real panel is in the basement."

Shane hands the binder full of the CCTV drives to Cece.

"Who knew this was here?" she asks.

"Just Maggie and Jenna. I guess you, too."

"Neither of you told anyone else?"

"No, but maybe I was followed," I say bitterly. There's a good chance I'm the reason Shane's shop was trashed. My feelings of guilt are slowly replaced by white-hot anger.

"From now on, we all need to be careful," Cece says. "It's a small town. People know you're looking into Tyler's case, Jenna... that you've spent time here." She bags the tape. "I'll put this with the other evidence. I doubt they have the nerve to break into a cop's house."

Cece texts the station. "I want you to stay with Maggie until this is over, okay?"

Shane brightens up. "Sure. That'd be awesome."

Chapter 19
Puzzle Pieces

Saturday morning is thrift shopping day. At least for Martha and Star, who woke up early to hunt for treasures in neighboring towns. So, I'm home alone with the cats and a plate of fresh pumpkin bread. The truth is, I could use a break. It's cold and clear outside, so I crack a window to get some fresh air, flick on a local news show out of Albany, and head for the kitchen. Martha left a pot of fresh coffee, so I pour a mug and cut a slice of the sweet, dense bread.

I try focusing on the program, but my mind keeps going back to the break-in at Shane's comic shop. Could Woody be so entitled he'd break in and trash the place looking for his stuff? If that's the case, what is so damn valuable that he would risk his career?

I go up to the spare bedroom, pull the box out from under the bed, and bring it downstairs to the dining room table. By the time I bring my bread and coffee in from the kitchen, I have to shoo Alex the cat off the top. I pull off the lid and rummage around. The stack of photos is sitting on top, so I flip through them.

There is an assortment of family photos: a wedding portrait of

Woody's parents, some pictures from a beach vacation when he and Abigail were grade school age, and toward the bottom, shots from high school dances, football games, and the annual Winter Festival. The pictures of Abby are heartbreaking, laughing and enjoying life, innocent of the fact there isn't much time left for her. I toss the stack on the table in frustration, startling Alex, who yowls, races off to safety, and kicks the whole pile off the table in the process.

"Sorry, buddy," I call after him. I need to ask Dave for tips on making a skittish cat feel more secure.

As I pick up the pictures, a cluster of photos I haven't seen fans across the floor. The shots are striking, with everyone dressed in black. The first is of Woody and Stockade in front of McGrath's Funeral Parlor, wearing dark suits and looking somber. The Spar brothers are standing to their left. To the far right, Audrey Vitner is barely in the frame. I remember the day. These are pictures from Coach Vitner's memorial service. How morbid. The entire town attended, including Mom and me. Tyler, of course, was in jail awaiting trial. I can't imagine how sad and frustrating that must have been for him. Tyler should have been there with his teammates, mourning the man they all loved.

There are a few more, mostly candid shots. One photo stands out. A group of Bell River High football players from every graduating class, arms linked in solidarity. I recognize the Spars in the center. Woody is obviously taking the picture, and Dylan is off to one side.

Behind the group, standing by the fence, a strange man is watching. I don't immediately recognize the guy and he doesn't seem like part of the crowd. I grab my phone and adjust my camera to the highest number of pixels before zooming in on his face. He's young, maybe in his twenties, with full lips, stringy hair, and acne. He has a large build and is wearing a combat jacket. He never went to Bell River High while I was there, that's for sure. There's something about his eyes, kind of detached. What really sticks out is the deadpan look on his face; his expression is flat, almost like he's made of wax. Probably just a relative, but I snap a picture and text Nadir anyway.

> Me: *Any chance you can ID this guy? Could be related to Joe or Audrey Vitner.*

The television interrupts my thoughts. The screen flickers with a banner that reads: *Weather Watch!* The anchor looks into the camera. "Stand by for a public warning from our reporter on the go, Rosa Gutierrez."

A pretty reporter wearing a chic but impractical white parka appears on-screen. She's standing on the Winter Bridge over-looking Bell River.

"Thank you, Jim. It's a beautiful winter day. But beware of danger. Bell River is experiencing an early thaw, and the ice is unstable. Many of you remember the day nine years ago, during similar conditions, when a group of teens was ice skating and the ice broke. I certainly do. I was one of those teens, and I survived. But my friend Abigail Teresa Wade, our Sheriff's daughter, did not."

The irony of the fact I'm holding funeral pictures during a newscast about the tragic fate of Abby Wade makes me sad. Such a horrible and terrifying way to die, trapped under the ice with no air. Poor Abby's death is like a wound this town can't seem to heal. Then there's the murder of Joseph Vitner and Tyler's conviction. Sometimes I wonder if Bell River isn't cursed.

Mom's cozy house suddenly feels claustrophobic. I stuff the photos back in the box, except the one with the strange man. Then I grab my coat and shove the picture into my pocket. There's one person I can think of who might be able to ID this "Waxman" guy, and she's just a short walk away.

Fifteen minutes later, I'm standing in front of Audrey Vitner's bright yellow house, my nose running from the cold, doubting my decision to show up unannounced. I planned to have answers for Coach's widow on my next visit, not more questions. I consider turning back, but my instinct tells me this is important. Besides, a quick look at the stranger in the photo will only take a minute of her time. The swing on the porch creaks as the chain sways in the wind. Before I can knock, her Yorkshire Terrier sounds the alarm.

"Hush, Barney," Mrs. Vitner says as she answers the door wearing flannel pajamas. Reading glasses hang from a string around her neck.

"Well, to what do I owe this surprise?" She narrows her eyes at me. "Do you have news?"

"No, Mrs. Vitner. I'm sorry." I force myself to make eye contact. "I have another question."

The terrier jumps on my leg as Mrs. Vitner decides between slamming the door in my face or inviting me in. "Go ahead." She stands firm in the doorway, arms crossed.

Clearly, I'm not getting inside.

"I'm sorry I have to show you this, but it could be important." I pull the photo from my pocket and point to Waxman. "Do you know this man?"

Grief washes over her features. "Why, that's my Joe's…"

"Memorial service," I finish her sentence. "Yes, it is. I wish there was an easier way."

She steadies herself on the doorframe and takes the photo.

"I remember, there were so many people. The whole town came."

"Your husband was well-loved." I point to the stranger again. "But do you recognize him? Is he a relative?"

She puts on her reading glasses and examines the photo. "What an odd-looking young man. He looks like one of those wax figures."

I nod in agreement. "I need to know if he's a family member. Or maybe a past teammate? Or someone who worked with your husband?"

"No. I've never seen him before. Not a family member or staff. And not on one of Joe's teams."

"You're sure?" I watch her reaction for a glimmer of recognition, but there's nothing.

"I'm more than sure. Joe kept a wall chart with the team's numbers and names. I've never seen this young man before." She hands me back the photo with sadness in her eyes. "Why do you ask? Does he have something to do with..." She trails off, unable to say the words.

"I'm not sure," I say, pocketing the photo. "Maybe. I had to check with you first."

"I see." Mrs. Vitner picks up her dog. "Will you find out who he is?"

"I will, even if I die trying."

"Good. And if that's all, I'd like to get back to my crossword." She closes the door before I can thank her.

Trudging to the sidewalk, I consider my mission a failure. I've upset Mrs. Vitner again and for nothing. Even though I'm no closer to figuring out who Waxman is, I know one thing, he's an outsider who didn't belong at that funeral.

The sky is still clear, but an icy wind has picked up, cutting through my layers of clothing. I consider calling Andy Barnes for a ride, but who knows how long that could take.

Walking briskly, blowing hot air on my mittened fingers, I hear an engine purr behind me. To my right, a dark blue Mercedes sedan slows down on the narrow road. My heart thuds in my chest as I quicken my pace. But the car stays even with me. When I hear the hum of a power window lowering, I pull off a mitten and slide my keys between my fingers to use as a weapon.

"Jenna? Is that you?"

At the sound of my name, I turn to see who it is. My fear melts and is quickly replaced by a nervous flutter in my stomach.

"Um. Hi, Dylan," I say through chattering teeth.

"You look like you're freezing," Dylan says, keeping pace with my stride.

"I'm fine." I keep walking. I haven't heard from Dylan since Cole crashed our date. I probably should have texted him an apology or an explanation, but Cole Braedon's weirdness threw me off. Besides, I was kind of hoping Dylan would make the first move.

"Do you need a ride?" He keeps rolling along next to me.

"No, I'm just getting some air."

"Are you sure? It's below zero. You look miserable. Oh! That's not what I meant."

Oh, screw it. He's right, why should I suffer? I turn toward the car.

He stops. I make my way to the passenger side.

"Thanks a lot." I try the door, but my fingers are numb.

He climbs out, opens the passenger side, and closes the door behind me. I'm enveloped by delicious waves of warmth. As he gets back in behind the wheel, I try to think of how to broach the subject of our ruined date. Thankfully, he brings it up first.

"Listen, Jenna, I'm so sorry about the other night. I shouldn't have stormed out. I wanted to call, but I was embarrassed."

"I'm sorry about Cole. He can be impossible at times." I rub my hands together.

"It's okay. Can I buy you a coffee? It'll warm you up." He flashes his easy, charming smile.

A tingle of excitement touches the back of my neck.

"That would be great."

Bean River Roasters is two blocks from Mom's duplex. The small brick corner shop opened in the mid-nineties when designer coffee first became popular and the town was still thriving. The business has changed hands multiple times and tried incorporating every trend, from wheat grass to acai bowls to Macha smoothies and even an open mic night, to no avail. The one constant that's kept the place open through economic ups and downs is good coffee and a cozy atmosphere.

As Dylan and I step inside, a rush of warm air infused with the aroma of fresh-brewed coffee envelops us. This is the first time I've been to Roasters, as locals call it, in years, and it's exactly as I remember. The mismatched furniture is plush and comfy, the lighting soft and flattering, and the coffee smells divine.

After receiving our order, Dylan and I gravitate to a well-worn couch in front of a bookcase full of dog-eared paperbacks. On a low table next to us is a half-completed jigsaw puzzle of kittens in a basket. I shrug off my coat and cradle my mocha latte, letting the enormous bowl-like mug warm my hands. Dylan hangs his jacket up before angling his body toward me and stirring three sugar packets into his cappuccino. He takes a small sip.

"Wow, that's good." He sets his mug down on the wooden table.

I sip my latte. "Maggie and I used to hang here on the weekends."

"Reading those doorstop novels." Dylan laughs. "I'm so glad we ran into each other, Jenna. I didn't know how to break the ice after the other night."

"Me too…" Just like on our date, Dylan's deep brown eyes focus on mine like I'm the only person in the room. My pulse instantly quickens. Maybe there is hope for this budding attraction.

"So, you said Cole's a colleague? Like a detective?"

"Kind of. He's also a friend and actually a pretty good guy. He just doesn't have the best social skills."

"No kidding." Dylan raises an eyebrow. I can't help but smile.

"He's helping me with Tyler's case," I add.

"That makes sense." Dylan relaxes into the soft couch. "Is that why he's in Bell River?"

"Actually, he was working on something else, up in Albany. But he's gone now." I take a drink of hot, chocolatey latte and feel myself warming up from the inside out.

"Well, I have to admit, I'm kinda glad he's gone." Dylan says in a soft voice. "How is it going, anyway, looking into everything?"

A lot of regular people—people who don't spend their lives surrounded by crime—have trouble talking about things like prison and murder. But I know what Dylan is asking, and I appreciate it.

"A case is like that puzzle." I gesture to the half-formed basket of kittens. "You just have to keep pushing the pieces around until they fit."

He nods and sips his drink.

"Is that what you were doing out in this weather? Pushing pieces?"

"I went to show Audrey Vitner a photo. Walking seemed like a good idea at the time. I forgot how brutal the wind can be here, even when the sun is out."

"What kind of photo?" Dylan says, puzzled.

My mind flashes to the memorial. Dylan was there. Maybe he knows Waxman.

"Actually, you were at Coach Vitner's memorial." I set down my mug and reach into my jacket pocket. I hand him the photo. "Do you recognize this guy?"

"Which one?"

I point at Waxman. "There, by the fence."

Dylan studies the picture. "I don't think I've ever seen this guy. Mrs. Vitner didn't know him?"

"Nope. No idea." I set the photo on the table between us.

"Where did you get the picture?" Dylan leans in, hooked on the mystery.

"Some of Woody's old photos got mixed up in a box of Star's stuff."

His expression softens. "Oh Jenna, I can't believe I haven't asked. How is Star doing?"

"She's fine, better actually." There he goes, surprising me again. He's so sweet. After the parade of crazy guys I've dealt with over the years, he's like a real grown-up.

"That's good. So why don't you just ask Woody about your mystery man?"

I like the way Dylan's mind works. He can be genuinely concerned but also stay focused on practical matters.

"It's complicated," I explain. "He locked down Star's bank account, and now she's keeping his stuff for leverage."

"Good for her. Woody's my friend, but his behavior at dinner the other night was out of order. So what're you going to do if you find this guy?"

"Ask him some questions about the night Tyler was arrested."

"Maybe I can help. I could see if anyone remembers the weirdo by the fence." He smiles and sips his cappuccino.

"Waxman, that's what I call him." I forward the image I snapped earlier.

Dylan's phone pings. He stares at Waxman's face. "It's kind of exciting helping to clear someone's name." He looks up at me shyly. "Is that weird?"

"Not at all. That's why I got into criminology. Solving a puzzle is exhilarating."

"Jenna?" He touches my hand lightly and my mouth is suddenly dry.

"Yes?" I manage to whisper.

"I know you won't be in town forever. I meant what I said about seeing each other again. I'm in New York City...often."

He looks at me intensely. A girl could melt into those eyes.

Then my phone chimes, startling both of us.

Star: *Urgent! Something here you need to see.*
Me: *Now?*
Star: *ASAP*
Me: *Be right there.*

"Is everything okay?" Dylan looks at me inquisitively.

"I've got to go. Star found something. She's putting the pieces together."

"I'll drive you."

"No, finish your coffee. It's a five-minute walk."

"Okay then. Go. Don't forget this." He hands me the photo. "I'll invite Woody for a beer and see if he remembers this Waxman guy."

Dylan leans in and gives me a soft kiss on the lips, which sends a warm tingle all the way to my knees. I grab my coat and dash back out into the cold.

This better be good, Star.

Chapter 20
Stake Out

It's a short walk to Martha's duplex. Even though I can see my breath, I feel warm from my exchange with Dylan Connor. How did I ever misjudge him so badly? Some guys would have ghosted me after Cole Braedon crashed our date, but not Dylan. He's patient and understanding. A little voice inside me sends up a warning: *Do not fall for this guy.* The timing is all wrong, and we live hundreds of miles apart.

I pull my scarf up against the icy wind and pick up my pace. Star's been through a lot. Whatever she found out must have made her nervous. I race up the driveway. The front door opens before I even reach the steps.

Star stands in the doorway, bundled up in an oversized sweater, holding a mug of tea. I recognize Martha's therapeutic answer to stressful events—bundle up and drink tea.

"Were you followed?" Star says nervously.

"I think we're safe." I bite my lip. Snarky remarks won't help.

Star's shoulders relax. She steps aside, letting me into the warm house. In the dining room, the contents of the box from Woody's house are spread over the table. Martha looks at me with a warning in her eyes, her hand resting on a teapot covered with a gingham cozy.

"Darjeeling?" she says and pours me a cup. Then she dollops in a spoonful of honey.

"Thanks." A slice of orange floats to the top. The concoction smells heavenly.

"I found this." She holds up a football-shaped keychain. Then pulls apart the two halves of the plastic ball to reveal a hidden thumb drive. "Wait until you see what's on it."

Star slots the thumb drive into her laptop and turns the machine toward me.

I sit down and double-click on the icon. A list of documents organized by date springs onto the screen. The list of dates goes back to before Coach Vitner's murder.

"These look like receipts." I scan the dates—every two months.

"Pick one," Star says. "They're all the same."

I click on a document. It's a receipt from the Mígōng Chemical Manufacturing Company, Anhui Province, addressed to WTW at a P.O. box. There's a list of chemicals. As I scan the purchases, I see several substances I am only too familiar with—anabolic steroids.

"My God." I look at Star. "I guess WTW is—"

"Woodrow Taylor Wade," Star says miserably. "My EX-fiancé."

"So Woody was importing steroids?"

"I think so," Star says.

"These dates go back to high school." I remember what Stan Spar told Cole. The product has changed, but not the system... someone else decides what the people want.

I send the files to Cece's email. In the subject line, I write "New Evidence."

"Didn't the Spar brothers sell...weed?" Star cups her mouth and whispers as to shield Martha from "rough" talk.

"It's alright, dear. I know what weed is," Martha says.

"So, Woody used the Spar's network to distribute his steroids," I muse aloud. "But who's supplying this town with Happy Kat?"

"I don't know, dear," Martha says. "It all sounds very tawdry."

"This whole time, Woody's been part of a drug ring..." Star's voice cracks.

"Looks like it. I'll need to check out this P.O. box."

"What the hell is wrong with me?" Star's eyes well up with tears. "How did I pick this guy?"

Martha shoots me a withering glance. Now I've done it. Star's having an emotional crisis. I guess I could have been a little more delicate.

"It's not your fault," I offer lamely, trying to comfort her.

"Now, honey, don't blame yourself," Martha says, handing Star a tissue.

"How could I be so stupid?" Star sinks down on a chair and takes a deep, shuddering breath.

"He wasn't honest with you. You're not a mind reader, after all," Martha consoles her.

"Mom? Can you put this somewhere safe?" I hand her the thumb drive and go sit by Star.

"I know just the place, Jenna Bean. A secret stash no one can find."

I take Star's hands in mine. "What you did today is amazing—a real breakthrough. We just got closer to finding the answers that will help set Tyler free, okay?"

"You think so?" She smiles through her tears. Even with her own life in tatters, Star brightens at the thought of helping her friends.

"Come on, Star," Martha says. "You've done enough detective work for one day." She motions toward me. "We're going to watch a romcom on Netflix tonight. Would you like to join us? I'm making popcorn."

"I would love to, but—" At that moment, my phone buzzes with the Peter Gunn ringtone I've assigned to a specific person. I look down at the text.

Cole: *Outside. Make sure you wear dark clothes.*
Me: *Give me 5.*

"I can't tonight. I have a stakeout."
"Suit yourself," Martha says.

A dark gray Chevy Sedan with a black interior pulls into the driveway, which is a surprising choice considering Cole's champagne tastes. I climb into the passenger seat.

"Chevy doesn't seem like your style." I point out.

"Gotta blend in." He smiles. "Not too many Maseratis in Bell River."

We drive through the quiet streets. The sun is nearly down, but unlike in my car, the heat works, and we are enveloped in a cloud of warmth. We arrive at the Spar's dead-end street. The neighborhood has seen better days. But still, it's hardly a place you'd imagine drug dealers living. The Spar Brother's gray, one-story house looks even worse at dusk. The last rays of sunshine only highlight the cracked paint and sagging wood.

According to our interrogation of the Spars, they always make the drop just before sunset. Cole parks and keeps the motor running. Sure enough, the Spars are true to their word. Jay and

Stan leave the house awkwardly, knowing they're being watched. They hop into Stan's green Challenger parked in the driveway and pull out.

"So far, so good." Cole follows, keeping his distance.

Ahead, they take a wide turn and pull up to the small post office at the edge of town. The counters are only staffed in the morning, but the outer lobby, where the P.O. boxes are located, is open to keyholders 24/7. Cole spot-checks the area before parking across the street under a tree to blend in with the shadows. From here, we have a good view of the glass-encased lobby.

Jay Spar opens the door with a key and walks directly to the correct box. He slides the envelope with the drug money inside and races back to the car like his pants are on fire.

The Spars drive off in a cloud of exhaust.

"Now what?" I sink down in my seat. "You think their connection will pick up the money tonight?"

"Maybe." Cole turns the engine off. You can see our breath floating in the air as the temperature drops. "Zip up. We might be here a while."

"By the way, look what Star found." I hand Cole my phone.

He examines the steroid receipts from China.

"No shit? The congressman wannabe?" Cole says. "Nice job."

"Do you think he's involved with the Happy Kat ring?"

"You grew up here, Jenna. What do you think?"

"I think there's a good chance. Like the Spars said, they kept selling whatever they were told. I doubt Woody is the mastermind, though. He was a straight-D student."

"How do you know that?"

"Everybody knows everybody in a town this size."

"You know, I come from a small town, too," Cole says, rubbing his hands together.

"Really? Where?" I try to rub my hands, but they're numb.

"I'm afraid that's classified," Cole says. "Here, let me help you." He takes my hands and lightly cups them. Then he leans in and breathes into the tent of his hand, creating heat. He smells like Sandalwood and expensive cigarettes. I feel the back of my neck tingle.

"That won't work," I say sternly.

"What do you mean, Jenna?" His searing green eyes are hypnotic.

"Stop trying to distract me."

Suddenly, I spot a black SUV driving down the street. The windows are tinted. "Cole, look," I whisper. "I think that's the same vehicle that tried to run me off the road."

The SUV pulls into the post office parking lot and sits idling. Cole grabs a pair of binoculars from the glove box.

"Those plates are from out of state. I'll bet when we run them, they're a dead end." He hands me the glasses, and I take a look.

The driver-side door opens, and an absolute monster of a human being steps out. He's well over six feet tall, wearing a black cap and a parka, and his arms look like ramrods about to burst his coat. His leg muscles bulge against his jeans. As he looks over his shoulder, I gasp. I recognize the pockmarked cheeks, flattened nose, thick lips, and gray, lifeless eyes, like a shark that crawled onto land.

"Holy crap, it's Waxman."

"You know him?" Cole says.

"No—not really. He was younger and thinner, but he was in a picture from Abby Wade's funeral."

"The kid that drowned. Interesting," Cole says. "I guess the waters run deep in Bell River."

"A pun? Really?" I elbow Cole and go back to watching the target.

Cole starts taking pictures with his phone as Waxman unlocks the lobby door, opens the P.O. box, and removes the envelope. He shoves the drug money into his coat pocket. Then he steps into the cold and climbs back into the SUV.

Cole waits for a beat before following. His fingers are like lightning, and my phone pings. He's already sent me his pictures of the drug drop.

"Don't say I never gave you anything." He grins and starts the engine. Then he slowly pulls out, letting Waxman get a head start.

"We can't risk him seeing us," I say, forwarding the pictures to Cece.

He laughs. "Don't nag, dear."

As always, Cole's driving is impressive. He weaves through the streets and past the town center, always staying out of sight. It becomes clear Waxman is headed for the prominent Bell River Estates on Pentecostal Road. The winding street is heavy with snow drifts, and Cole is careful to hang back. Finally, just before the border of Eastmoor County, the SUV turns up a long driveway.

Cole drives past and pulls into a neighboring driveway with a For Sale sign at the entrance. He shuts off the headlights and slowly moves into position.

As Waxman parks at the end of a small fleet of black SUVs, we have a clear view of a large house and fenced grounds. Then he climbs out of his vehicle with the envelope and walks up the steps of a vast stone mansion with a heavy wooden door. He rings the bell.

"Do you know the house?" Cole looks through the binoculars.

I shake my head. "I don't know anyone in this part of town."

I take my phone out, zoom in, and start recording as the porch lights flick on. The door opens and the vague outline of a man stands in the doorway, framed by the light.

Waxman hands him the drug money.

"Do you recognize him?" Cole says.

I zero in on the handoff and adjust the lens. As the man steps into the porchlight, I have a clear view. I can't believe what I'm seeing.

"Yes, and it's not Woody."

"Who then?" Cole says.

"It's his asshole father—Sheriff Woodrow 'Stockade' Wade."

Chapter 21
Midnight Surprise

By the time Cole glides the car down the long, dark driveway, Waxman is gone. Scanning both directions, the road is empty, without a spark of headlight or a trace of exhaust, just asphalt and the dark forest blanketed by snow. The guy has disappeared as if he were a ghost.

"He must know the back roads," I point out uneasily. "There are a dozen side roads up and down Pentecostal. He could have taken any one of them."

"He's in the wind for now," Cole says. "Let's get you home."

As we drive back to Martha's house, Cole's mood is light. He turns on the radio to a Sirius radio art pop station and hums along to the weirdest song I've ever heard, one that makes Portishead sound commercial. I sink into the car seat and let the moody music envelop me. The sight of Stockade Wade taking drug money has left me disconcerted. Suspecting the sheriff is corrupt was one thing. Knowing he's part of the Happy Kat drug ring is something else entirely.

"What's wrong?" Cole says. "That expression you get on your face is tragic."

"What expression?" I glance at him in the thin light from the dashboard.

"Somewhere between I ate a briny pickle and lactic acid build-up." He smirks, then pulls out one of his expensive black cigarettes and cracks the window. "You don't mind, do you?"

"Would it matter if I did?" I lower my own window an inch.

"You should be happy, Jenna. We've made a dent in this case."

"I just find it hard to believe Stockade Wade is a drug kingpin. He's so, I don't know, small town."

"More likely Wade is working for the kingpin. Criminals corrupt people, Jenna. And that sheriff is corrupt. Wouldn't be hard to entice him into all sorts of nefarious business." He takes a drag off his cigarette, pleased with himself. "You aren't feeling sorry for that jackass?"

"No, it's just that this case is bigger than I thought. It's about more than my brother. Maybe we should contact the authorities—"

"I am the authorities." Cole laughs. "Listen, Jenna. Wade doesn't know you're onto him, and that puts you in a good position."

"What is that supposed to mean?"

"Just that your internship gives you a front row seat inside the organization. When you're around Wade, keep your eyes peeled. But play dumb."

"Play dumb? I'm not sure how to do that."

"You know, try not to be such a smartass."

"Just because I've outsmarted you a few times."

Cole laughs. "Just pretend you're clueless. Things are getting dangerous. It's all connected. We just can't see how yet. First, your brother was set up. Then you start poking around, and the warehouse burns down. Now the Wades are involved in a drug ring. The case is heating up...no pun intended."

"Meaning what?"

"An investigation is like a crucible. If the perps think you know something, this is about the time somebody gets killed. And I don't want that to be you."

Cole glances over at me with his intense green eyes. His gaze makes me nervous, so I look out the window. Here on the back roads, it's desolate, there are no streetlights, and we're surrounded by woods. Let's face it: Upstate New York is someplace murderers go to dump bodies never to be found.

"Alright," I say. "But I'm not playing dumb with Cece or Maggie—they're my colleagues. They deserve to know what we've learned."

"Fair enough." Cole smiles as he pulls up to Martha's house. He leans over and unclips my seat belt, then reaches up and gently tucks a loose hair behind my ear. "And remember, beautiful, I'm just a phone call away."

"Good to know." I open the car door, welcoming the rush of cold air on my skin.

"I'll try to ID Waxman. And you're going to—" He looks at me expectantly.

"Play dumb," I say sweetly, stepping out into the snow.

Cole pulls away, and I watch his taillights disappear into the cold, dark night.

The duplex is quiet, so I circle to the back door to avoid setting off Mrs. Dupont, who I suspect sits up until all hours with a pair of binoculars. Opening the screen door, my fingers guide the key into the keyway. The cheap door swings open. The lock is a basic spring latch you could pop with a credit card. A flash of glowing eyes startles me. The cats are up and restless. I pat Eliza's head as I tiptoe around her.

Before I reach the stairs, there's a creaking noise. I freeze for a second. Is someone up in the middle of the night? Martha heading for the bathroom? Then, I distinctly hear weight shifting in the upstairs hallway. That's too heavy to be Martha. My heart speeds up. Cole's words echo in my mind. This is about the time when someone gets killed. I estimate where the sound is coming from. Creaking footsteps are headed toward the room where Star is sleeping. My instinct is to run up the stairs, but that's not a good idea. They'll hear me coming, and I have no idea about the size of my opponent.

Instead, I call Cece. After two rings, she answers. "This better be good."

"There's an intruder at my mom's house," I whisper. "Hurry."

"On my way," Cece says. "Don't do anything stupid."

I silence the ringer on my phone and slip off my winter coat. Then, I take the knife Cole gave me out of my jeans pocket and flick open the blade. There's the creaking again. The intruder is almost at Star's door. Cece said not to be crazy, but I can't leave Star alone.

Slowly, carefully, I take the stairs, holding the knife in a reverse grip. I review my Krav Maga. Defend and attack at the same time. Fight with aggression. Never go down.

As I start down the hallway and my eyes adjust to the dark, I freeze. There's a hulking figure standing in Star's doorway. The intruder silently turns the handle and pulls out a length of wire.

Oh God. Is he going to strangle her?

Despite his size, the intruder moves fluidly toward Star's bed as he stretches the wire between his hands. She rolls on her side and pushes herself up.

"Jenna? Is that you?" Star whispers uncertainly.

I slip into the room and flick on the lights. The intruder whips around, holding the wire. Even though he's wearing a ski mask, his bulging muscles are familiar. I'd bet my life this is Waxman.

"Get away from her!" I hold the knife out in a defensive stance. The intruder steps back, startled. A siren blares in the distance.

"Hear that? The cops are on the way. Who are you?" I demand.

The intruder growls and rushes me, trying to hook my neck with the wire. But as he raises his arms, I bob and weave, avoiding his deadly bear hug. Then I slash upward, grazing his bicep as the knife finds its mark and slices across his cheek. He roars with surprise.

"You fucking bitch!" the intruder yells in a gravelly voice. He holds his wounded face with one hand. Then he runs down the hallway, thudding and crashing into furniture. As soon as the front door slams, my shoulders sink in relief.

"My God, Jenna." Star runs over and hugs me. "Y-you attacked that man."

I pull Star to the window. A dark figure runs across the snow and disappears into the tree line just as Cece's police cruiser pulls into the driveway.

"Better get dressed," I tell Star. "You'll need to make a statement."

Downstairs, I hear Martha open the front door, and Cece scrape her snowy boots on the welcome mat. I step onto the landing. Cece looks up, her eyes wide. Only then do I realize I'm still holding the knife like a crazy person. A wave of fatigue rushes over me as the adrenaline subsides.

"Jenna Bean, are you alright?" Martha says nervously.

"Yes, fine, sorry." I close the knife and walk downstairs. "There's blood—"

"I can see that." Cece pulls out an evidence bag. "A William Henry? That's a damn fine weapon."

"It was a gift." I drop the knife in the bag.

"We'll swab for DNA." She seals the bag and tucks the evidence in her jacket pocket. "I'll have this back to you tomorrow."

"Good grief, you had a knife fight?" Martha is slowly putting the pieces together. "I heard a commotion. I thought you and Star were watching an action movie."

"Jenna saved me, Mrs. Stack," Star says, racing down the stairs. "She was amazing."

"Sure looks that way." Cece raises an eyebrow. "Jenna? Step outside for a moment?"

I grab my coat and we walk out onto the cold porch. The drop in temperature helps me focus and shake off the shock.

"Alright, what happened." Cece is all business.

I pull the photo of Waxman at Abigail Wade's funeral up on my phone.

"See this guy? He broke in here tonight and tried to kill Star. I'm sure it was him."

"Who is he?"

"I don't know. I've been calling him Waxman."

"Why would this...Waxman try to kill Star?"

"She knows too much."

Cece looks skeptical. "About what?"

"The case. We all do." I scroll through my phone to the stake out pictures. "We followed Waxman earlier."

"You and your FBI friend?"

"Yes. First, he picked up drug money from the Spar's mail drop. Then, he went to Pentecostal Road." I show her the video of Stockade Wade taking the drug money.

"Well, I can't say I'm surprised, but this changes everything." She paces. "We need to keep this tight. You, me and Maggie for now. If Stockade Wade finds out you have this—"

"Have what? I don't know anything. Some weirdo tried to break in. He was wearing a mask."

Cece grins. "Then let's take some statements."

As we return to the warm house, the back door opens. Mrs. Dupont storms inside with her hair tucked into a turban, wearing a fuzzy pink bunny robe and slippers.

"Martha? Martha! There's a police car out front. Again!"

"Everything's fine, Annie," Martha says. "Officer Myers, this is Mrs. Dupont."

"Hmmpf. It's about time you got here. I saw a man run into the woods. He could have killed Martha." Annie's mouth flutters with emotion, and she looks overwhelmed.

Martha puts an arm around Annie's shoulders.

"Come on, dear, let's make tea. It's going to be a long night."

Chapter 22
The Lab

Between Mrs. Dupont's endless questions and Martha's fussing, Cece's investigation slows to a crawl. It's past midnight by the time I stretch out on the couch. Once my head hits the pillow, I descend into a restless sleep. Just before morning, I have a strange dream.

I'm standing under the Winter Bridge. Across the ice is a girl wearing a navy-blue coat, dark red mittens, and a wool hat with a reindeer pattern. She waves to me. Her face is familiar: big brown eyes and delicate, pensive lips. With a start, I recognize Abigail Wade.

"Abby?" I call across the frozen river and take a step toward her. The ice creaks ominously. Snow starts falling, piling against the bridge. Another step, and a crack spreads jaggedly across the surface. "I can't come any closer."

"Look underneath," Abby says in a hollow voice. She points to the ice.

I kneel, brushing the snow away. Underneath is an abyss of deep water. Something is moving down there. A body floats up from the bottom, hair swaying in the current. The frozen face turns to look at me with dead eyes—the face is mine.

I snap awake, breathing hard. My phone is buzzing.

"Stack here."

"Rise and shine," Detective Myers says. "Officer Pete and I are going to interview Karl Haben. Can you meet us at the lab in an hour?"

"Absolutely."

"Texting the address now.

I tiptoe upstairs to check on Star and change clothes. She's fast asleep, curled up like a kitten. Martha, on the other hand, is already up. Voices drift from the kitchen.

I dress quickly and head to the kitchen to grab coffee, leaving my jacket and messenger bag on a chair by the front door. Martha and Mrs. Dupont are huddled around the table, discussing last night's excitement.

"You'd think those police would be back here this morning to look for tracks," Annie says. "We pay their salaries, you know."

"It snowed last night," Martha explains. "Any tracks are probably gone."

"Well, we never had trouble like this before she—"

"Good morning," I interrupt.

Annie purses her lips and Mom pours me a cup of coffee.

I sip my drink. "Sorry about all of this trouble, Mrs. Dupont."

"Well, where are you off to now?" she answers testily.

"Meeting Detective Myers. We're going to get to the bottom of these...intrusions."

Mom gives me a warning look, not to set her landlady off.

"Taking action," Annie says, pleased. "That's more like it."

"Look, I've got to go but I texted Andy Barnes last night. He's going to come by and put deadbolts on all your locks."

Annie peers over her mug expectantly.

"Your place too, Mrs. Dupont." I toss my coffee back.

She manages a thin smile. "Well, that's very good of you dear."

On the way to my car, I text Andy Barnes.

Me: *Deadbolts at Annie Dupont's too please.*

I scrape ice off the windshield and climb into my old clunker. But when I start the engine, it turns over without igniting, endlessly cranking. Sounds like the alternator. Good luck finding that old part. I look at my watch. Damn it! I'm going to be late. The lab is located in an industrial park in the Scrublands. Not too far. I could call Andy for a ride. Then a thought occurs to me...

Isn't Tyler's old motorcycle in the garage? Martha's been tending to it like a talisman for the day Tyler is released.

I run inside the house, fish the key out of the hall drawer and change into my leather jacket and riding boots. "I'm taking the bike, Mom," I call out.

"Be careful," she answers. She knows me well enough not to try and stop me.

Before Annie Dupont can add her two cents, I'm out the door. I back the motorcycle out of the garage and kickstart the engine. It starts right up, and I'm relieved to see the studded tires for winter driving. The roads are slippery as I wind slowly through town.

The Winter Bridge is dead ahead. Steep snowbanks rise up on either side of the road. As I cross over the river, the ice reminds me of my dream.

The road to the lab is a twisting labyrinth, past non-descript one-story units. Cece's address ends at a rusted metal door. The police cruiser is parked nearby, but it's empty. I pull the bike around to the passenger side. The car door is ajar. Something's wrong.

I scan my surroundings. A black SUV with tinted windows is

parked on the far side of the lot. What the hell is going on? I roll the bike out of sight and follow muffled voices to a side window. What I see through the grimy glass stops my breath.

Inside the lab, Cece and Pete are on the floor, their wrists zip-tied, duct tape over their mouths. Pete's gun belt and Cece's holster lie on the counter. I sink down and press my back against the wall. Now what? Slowly, I peek through the glass again. This time Cece spots me. Her eyes are steely, and she tilts her head to indicate the far side of the counter. Deep in heated conversation are Waxman and Karl Haben.

For the first time, I get a good look at Waxman. There's a fresh slash mark across his cheek. I knew it! He's definitely the one who broke in last night. He has a thick neck and powerful shoulders. His skin is covered in scars and prison-style tattoos. He has a square face, a broken nose, and humorless lines etched along his mouth, down to his heavy jaw. His hair is thin and wispy, and he has a pair of cauliflower ears. The guy is a testosterone case, and fighting is second nature to him.

Carefully, I slide the window open to hear what they're saying.

"Orders from the top," Karl Haben says. "Wade's coming to deal with these two. They'll be killed in the line of duty."

"Hear that?" Waxman laughs in a raspy voice. "You're gonna be heroes."

"Then you need to take care of Simonsen and Stack. They know too much. And don't botch it this time."

So, Haben is in on it too. Cece and Pete must have surprised him and Waxman.

I signal to Cece and sneak back to the patrol car. Then I pop the trunk. There's an old Ithaca Model 37 Shotgun, a 12-gauge police special with ammo. I stay crouched down as I load the slugs into the rifle. At that exact moment, my phone buzzes.

Cole: *I made the funeral crasher. What did you call him...
Waxman? His name is Roy Pitts. Worked as a mercenary
overseas. Extremely dangerous. Stay clear of him.*
Me: *Too late...*
Cole: *What's that supposed to mean?*
Me: *I'm at Bell River Crime Lab. Pitts has Cece and Pete.*
Cole: *Don't do anything stupid!*
Me: *No time. But I am armed. Text you when it's over.*
Cole: *Check the floor plan.*

I text him the address of the lab. Then I turn my phone off and
pump a slug into the chamber. Moving around to the front of the
building, I try the door. It's locked. Next, I try each window. One
opens into a storage room. It's a tight fit, but I wedge my shoulder
through, climb inside, and land with a thump. I listen for the
sound of running feet—nothing. The door opens to an empty
passageway. I inch down the hall. This door should be the lab.
Silently, I turn the handle.

Pitts and Haben are still talking. I brace the police special
against my shoulder.

"Hands up where I can see them!" I shout.

They look up, startled. Then Pitts takes off running with the
speed of a weasel. On the far side of the lab is another door.

Crap! I guess Cole had a point about checking the floor plan.

Suddenly, a beaker explodes next to me, spraying me with
glass. The right side of my body stings. Pitts has a gun, and he's
shooting. I return fire as Pitts reaches the door. The rifle kicks into
my shoulder as lab equipment explodes in a hail of glass. But Roy
Pitts is already gone.

I turn to Karl Haben, who raises his hands slowly, watching me
with milky eyes.

"Un-tie them," I demand.

The floor is covered in shattered glass as Karl Haben bends over Cece. His scalpel glints in the winter light streaming through the window.

"Be careful," I warn, aiming the rifle at his head. "One slip, and you're dead."

"Alright, alright..." Haben watches me with one eye as he slides the scalpel against Cece's zip tie. With a flick of his wrist, he cuts through the plastic. Hands free, Cece peels the duct tape off her mouth and takes the scalpel from Haben.

"Good job, rookie." Cece nods to me as she frees Officer Pete.

He rips the duct tape off his mouth quickly, leaving a rectangular patch of red skin.

"I'm allergic to latex." He coughs violently and spits. "Damn it all, this town has gone crazy."

"Welcome to the party, Pete," Cece says, rubbing her wrists. She fastens her gun holster before pulling on her jacket. Pete puts on his utility belt and checks his gun.

"I had nothing to do with this fiasco," Haben says, looking at the floor.

A white-hot spark of anger lights up inside me as I process the facts. This is the guy who condemned my little brother to hell. I point the rifle at the center of Haben's chest.

"How can you say that?" I demand. "You faked the evidence that convicted my brother."

"She's only an intern." Haben wrings his hands nervously. "She has no idea what she's talking about."

Cece shoots me a warning look before gently prying the rifle from my fingers. "I don't know, Karl. I think the intern may have a point. Let's start with your friend. Who was that guy?"

Haben shakes his head. "If I talk, I'm dead."

"According to my contact, his name is Roy Pitts," I offer. "He's a mercenary."

Haben's eyes widen, and his jaw goes slack. "How did you—"

"And I'd say that cut on his face puts him at your mom's last night," Cece adds. "Thank your source for the ID. Now, Karl, you're looking at time in prison. I can read you your rights—"

"No! I won't be safe," Haben pleads. "This whole thing goes higher than you can possibly know."

"Higher than Stockade Wade? Isn't he the head of the Happy Kat ring?" I prompt him, watching for his reaction.

"My God, you really have no idea, do you?" There's terror in Haben's eyes. Sweat beads along his brow. "You've got to help me."

A red dot appears in the center of Karl Haben's forehead, wavering like a flame. I stare at it, mesmerized for a second.

"Get down!" I scream, but it's too late.

A window shatters, spraying more glass across the room. The red point on Haben's forehead darkens and spreads like ink on soft paper as the bullet pierces his brain. He stands stiff, eyes vacant. Then, gravity pulls him to the earth with a heavy thud. Blood spreads under his head.

"Oh hell," Pete says, breathing hard. He pulls his gun out, holding it tight by his cheek. We all sink behind the counter. Outside, tires screech.

Peering through the splintered windowsill, I see the black SUV peel away, cutting dirty tracks in the snow. "Pitts! He's getting away!"

Cece's already on the radio calling for backup.

"Eastmoor City PD! Shots fired. Requesting back up, an ambulance, and forensics. Location: Bell River Crime Lab. Also—I need a bolo on Roy Pitts, P-I-T-T-S. Six foot two, medium hair, tattoos, driving a black SUV, armed and dangerous. Approach with caution." She turns to Pete. "Watch the door. Haben said Wade was on his way. I don't want any more surprises."

I look over at Karl Haben, sprawled on his back, eyes open,

staring blankly at the ceiling. How did a respected forensic scientist get involved in all of this?

I shake off the shock and set aside my questions. No time to process now. "I need to find Star. Pitts has a head start."

Cece hesitates for a moment. I can see she's worried about me. Then she hands me her gun. "I'll dispatch Eastmoor police to Martha's. Meet them there. And don't take any chances."

Chapter 23
The Winter Bridge

Snow has started to fall, and the sky is a soft gray. I tuck the gun into the motorcycle's saddlebag and phone Star. She's not picking up. Next, I call Martha, but it goes straight to voicemail. I don't have Mrs. Dupont's number.

I zip up my leather jacket and pull on my helmet. Then I kick-start the bike and a plume of blue smoke, along with a strong gas smell, eject from the engine. My imagination catches fire as I wind my way back to the main road. What if Roy Pitts is already at Mom's house? No, that's impossible. He'd never make it across town that quickly, even with a head start and flooring it.

As I pull onto the highway, the wind is howling, scattering snow flurries across the road. The cold air cuts through my leather jacket and my gloved fingers begin to feel numb.

Before I reach the Winter Bridge, a vehicle pulls behind me about a mile back. I don't think anything at first. Then I see it's a black SUV, and the hackles rise on my neck.

Is that Roy Pitts? Did he wait for me?

"Damn!" I say aloud. I force the bike to go faster, pushing my luck on the snowy road as the SUV speeds up, growing larger in my side mirror. The barren fields covered in snow are whipping past me in a blur. A car approaches in the opposite lane. I try to wave them down, but they drive past. A desperate sense of isolation and helplessness swells up in my throat. I can't stop. I can't go faster. I can't get to my phone. I'm alone with no way to call for help. The road rumbles under my tires, but the wheels are not sticking to the road, and the faster I push the bike, the more nerve-racking the ride becomes.

As the SUV closes in, I'm dwarfed by its size. The front grill looms over my back as the weight of the truck rocks behind me. I try to make out the driver, but the glass is tinted. I can't see a damned thing. The driver guns the motor. I have no choice but to go too fast on the slippery road. The bike shudders unsteadily. A shock jolts through my freezing hands. I clench my teeth, forcing myself to stay steady. If I overreact to any movement, I'm dead.

Up ahead is the Winter Bridge. Snow blows under the arch and piles on the abutments. As I barrel toward the rising road, I'm forced to slow down. The SUV guns its engine and butts up against my bumper. That's when I see the ice just ahead, rushing toward me. The wet snow has frozen into a slick patch, and I'm headed right for it. As my front tire hits the ice, there's a sudden strange, feeling of detachment. The motorcycle hydroplanes, moving eerily sideways across the lane before slamming into a massive snow-bank. Everything goes black.

~

I wake up to the biting cold. My head is foggy, and one leg is wedged under the motorcycle. I try to lift the bike, but my left shoulder bursts with pain. Snow falls in wet clumps as I pull my helmet off with my good arm. I check for broken bones. Thankfully, my limbs are intact. I hit the ground hard enough to sprain the hell out of my shoulder and to bruise...badly. Twenty feet away, the black SUV is idling on the other side of the snowbank. I can barely make out the occupant as he steps out of the SUV, holding a rifle. Then I hear a familiar voice, low and gruff. He clears his throat and spits on the ground.

"Now look what you've gone and done," Stockade Wade says. "I knew you Stack kids were trouble." Snow crunches under the sheriff's boots as he stops, cocks his gun, and drops a slug in the chamber. I try to lift the bike again, but the wheel is jammed deep in the snow drift, pressing down on my leg. I get some leverage and heave, rocking the handlebars back and forth to free myself. But the bike barely moves an inch.

Stockade Wade strolls toward me, hat tilted low over his eyes, gun casually butted up against his shoulder. I hold my breath and slam my good arm up with all of my strength. Despite the jolt of pain, my leg starts to work free from under the frame, but I'm out of time. I reach for the saddlebag with Cece's gun inside. My fingers stretch and touch the leather. But before I can get the gun, Wade's head peers over the snowbank and he swings the rifle up, pointing the business end at my chest.

"Come out of there," Wade orders. His eyes are black pits, remorseless and cold.

"How're you going to explain shooting me?" I challenge him. "An injured, unarmed person on the side of the road?"

"Good point." Wade turns the gun around and holds the barrel like a club. "I'll just say you crashed your bike and hit your head on the cement." He climbs over the snowbank in his police issue parka. I don't doubt for a minute that he'll crush my skull with that heavy gun.

"Cece will know. She'll come after you."

"Not if it looks like an accident." He stands over me and cocks his head. "Maybe I'll even do a little mouth to mouth to make it look good."

"You're a monster." Repulsed, I push backward, trying to get away from him.

"Wait, isn't that the same motorbike your brother rode the night Joe Vitner died?"

"You mean the night Roy Pitts murdered Vitner and you framed Tyler?"

"Clever girl." Wade lifts the rifle butt above my head. "Ironic, don't you think?"

Before he can slam the weapon down, I kick him with my free leg hard in the knee. He topples into the snowbank. Then, heaving with all my might, I free my pinned leg. My jeans rip as I scramble upright and run. But I'm too close to the steep riverbank, and my feet slide out from under me. I tumble down the rocky hill to the frozen river, hitting a thicket of dead cattails sticking out of the frozen ground. Covered in scratches, I push through the wet snow, clothes sodden, weighing me down. With my good arm, I pull my phone out of my pocket, but there's no service.

"Damn it," I say under my breath. Trudging along the riverbank, I head for the distant trees. The ice seems solid at the river's edge, but further out, in the center where the water is deep, chunks of ice bob on the surface.

Wade lumbers down the snowy embankment, following me in his heavy boots.

"Nowhere to run to, Jenna," he calls out, and stops to fire a warning shot.

The bullet explodes at my feet, kicking clumps of ice and snow into the air. The shot echoes and a murder of crows takes flight. They cackle and make a hollow rattling noise as I climb over the

scattered rocks on the river's shore. The snow is deep, and my footprints form a clear trail for Wade to follow.

As I round the bend, a fallen cottonwood tree blocks my path. I
stop, trying not to panic. The trunk is massive, the roots tangled up
in the sky. The tree must have broken the ice early in the winter
because it's frozen solid and half in the river. I search for an escape
route, but there's no way around the tree. The only solution is to
walk out onto the ice. I stay close to the trunk as I tread carefully
onto the frozen river. The ice creaks under my feet, threatening to
break. If I can just work my way around the trunk, there will be
something between me and that gun.

I'm making progress, getting farther out on the ice, but closer
to safety. Just another ten feet or so, and I can get around the tree
and back to the riverbank.

Then behind me, comes the sound of a rifle being pumped.

"I've got you." Wade's voice is low and menacing.

I turn around with my hands up and face the sheriff.

"I've got pictures of you accepting drug money from Roy Pitts."

"Then I guess that makes you a witness." Stockade Wade
laughs, squinting through his gun sights. "Why'd you have to
come back here anyway? You must've known you can't win. I'm
the law in Eastmoor County."

"You put my brother in prison to cover your drug business. I
couldn't let that stand."

"You've got it all wrong." Wade shakes his head. "There are
bigger forces at work here."

"What forces?" Slowly, I back up on the ice. If I can keep him
talking, maybe I can buy some time. Then I remember Stockade
Wade's weakness. His ego. "What about your legacy? I remember
Abby used to call you her hero."

"Shut up!" His eyes narrow and I can see his hands shake.

"What would she say about the man you've become?"

"You have no idea what you're up against. How could you know? You're just a stupid girl."

Wade squeezes the trigger, but at the last second, he flinches. The bullet grazes my injured arm and slices through my leather jacket. There's a loud cracking sound and a crisscross pattern appears on the ice. I try to stay as still as possible, cradling my bleeding arm. I've hit a nerve in Wade, so I keep pushing. Maybe I can rattle him enough that he'll make a mistake.

"Where did Abby die? Just there, wasn't it?" I point out on the ice. "I remember now. You came to look for her, but it was too late."

"Damn you." Wade aims the gun again, face red with anger. Then something changes in him, he looks confused. "Did you hear that?"

"Hear what?" I inch back along the tree.

"I could have sworn—" The sheriff looks out at the frozen lake. Snow swirls across the surface of the ice, forming a loose vortex— a snow devil. The wind moans, a faint sound, almost like a girl's voice. Then Wade starts to walk out onto the ice as if in a trance. Distantly, I see something unexplainable: a girl standing on the river, wearing a reindeer hat and red mittens. Her voice floats on the wind, thin and sweet. A chill rushes through me.

"What the hell..." I whisper and shake my head. When I look again, there's only the swirling snow devil moving over the river in a slow dance.

Wade calls out. "Abby? Is that you?" The sheriff lurches forward, eyes fixed on the whirling snow. The ice creaks and strains under his weight.

"Watch out!" I cry, faintly, then louder. "Stop!"

But it's too late. With a loud crack, the ice breaks and Wade drops into the black water like a stone. The water bubbles for a moment where he fell before the ice closes over and the hole disappears. The snow devil evaporates in a rush of scattering wind. I try to reach the spot where Wade went under, but the river groans and threatens. Slowly, carefully, I back away, past the tree to solid ground, leaving a trail of blood behind me.

Chapter 24
Marker 27

As I reach the riverbank, an eerie stillness descends. There are no birds singing, no crows cawing, no creatures rustling in the frosty grass or trees. It's as if nature can sense the end of a life. I'm shaking, overcome with horror, and my eyes sting with tears. But it's hard to tell if I'm crying for Stockade Wade or with relief that he's gone.

Slowly, I make my way to the riverbank. I'm in bad shape. My arm is throbbing, and there's a nick where the bullet ripped my jacket, leaving a trail of red drops on the ice. My kneecaps are scraped and bloodied, and I'm limping. Every step hurts as I trudge back through the snow. When I reach the steep slope by the bridge, I break the ice with a stick and pull myself back up to the highway. Finally, exhausted and muscles aching, I collapse next to Tyler's bike.

I lay in the snow for a moment, staring at the sky. It's a miracle I made it back. Pulling out my phone, I try to get a signal, but at this point, it's only a ritual. There's no service.

Tangled on the motorcycle's handlebars, my scarf flutters in the wind. I slip my injured arm out of my sleeve and use the scarf as a tourniquet, pulling the end tight with my teeth. Then I start digging the bike out of the snow. Once the bike is upright, I try kickstarting the motor. The engine cranks but won't catch. Damn it! I'm soaking wet, and my fingers are starting to go numb. There's no other choice. I'm going to have to walk back to town.

Then, in the distance, a car appears, coming closer.

Seeing a sign of civilization should be comforting, but it's not. After all those cryptic warnings from Stockade Wade, I feel uneasy. I pull Cece's gun out of the saddlebag and crouch behind a snowbank. The car slows down next to Wade's SUV and the slush I've made trying to start the bike. Then I recognize the dark blue Mercedes and breathe a sigh of relief.

Dylan Connor pulls over and leaves the car running. My blood trail leads to the bike. He steps halfway out the driver's side door and calls out.

"Hello? Anyone there? Is everything okay?"

I tuck the gun in my coat pocket and step out.

"Boy, am I glad to see you." I limp toward him.

"Jenna?" Dylan says, surprised. Then he sees my tattered state. "You're hurt!" He rushes over and slips his arm around me. "Are you okay?"

"I'm fine." I show him my arm. "There's been an accident."

"You look pretty banged up. Did you crash that bike?"

Now that Dylan's here and I'm safe, the whole ordeal seems unbelievable. I take a few breaths and try to find the words. It's all so crazy. I point at the frozen river. The hole is long gone and covered with snow, as if watching Wade fall into the cold, black water was just a dream. And there's no way I'm admitting to seeing Abigail Wade's ghost.

"Stockade Wade fell through the ice. I think he's dead."

"The sheriff?" Dylan says, looking into the distance. "What was he doing out there?"

"Chasing me." My teeth start chattering.

"Chasing you?" Dylan eyes narrow with concern. "My God. We better call the cops."

"There's no service." I hold up my phone. "I tried."

"I've got a satellite phone." He gently steers me toward his car. I'm shaking with cold as he holds the door open. "Better get inside and warm up."

"Okay." I climb in, grateful and relieved. The engine is running, and the heat envelops me. I slip the rest of the way out of my wet, bloodied jacket and clutch it on my lap. The coat is ruined, but right now, it's evidence I was stalked and shot.

Dylan takes the satellite phone from the glove compartment and stands outside so the signal can connect. He dials a number, and I listen to his muffled voice as I sink into the soft leather seat.

"Yes, there's been an accident. The sheriff fell through the ice. We're at the mile twenty-seven marker." He hangs up and slides into the car next to me. "They'll be here in ten minutes." He points to my makeshift tourniquet. "Does it hurt?"

"Stings a little. But I'm just grazed."

"I think you're in shock, Jenna." Dylan pulls off his wool coat and lays it over me like a blanket. Then he takes my hands to warm them. "What happened out there?"

"Wade was...hunting me." Even as I say it aloud, my story sounds far-fetched. "He chased me onto the ice."

"Sheriff Wade?" Dylan squeezes my hand. "Why would he do that?"

I catch my reflection in the side mirror. I'm a mess: dead twigs and clumps of snow are tangled in my hair. There's a gray smear across my cheek.

"Because I—"

A car pulls up behind us. I check the mirror, expecting a police car, but it's a black SUV. For a moment, I'm confused. Then, a large man wearing a baseball cap and parka climbs out. Snow crunches under his feet as he walks toward Dylan's car. There's a red slash across the cheek—a slash I made. My heart races. It's Roy Pitts.

"Oh my God," I gasp in fear. "We've got to get out of here!"

Dylan glances in the rearview mirror before looking at me.

He smiles reassuringly. "Not so fast, Jenna."

"Dylan, we have to go!"

He lowers the window and gestures for Pitts to come forward.

"I'm sorry," Dylan says. "I wish it hadn't come to this, But you're so damned tenacious."

"You?" I say, eyes wide. "My God, you ordered Vitner's murder."

"Looks like it." Dylan smiles, but his eyes are distant.

"You're behind the Happy Kat ring?" I'm stunned, but it tracks. Dylan knows all the players and can use the fact he manages his family's properties as a cover.

"Now you're catching on." Dylan nods at Roy Pitts, who looms outside my window, grinning.

The reality of my situation hits me. Sweet, caring Dylan is a murderer, and I'm stranded on a country road with two monsters. My mind is racing.

"Don't act so shocked, Jenna. I'm a businessman, and drugs are a growth industry."

"What about my brother? What was he? Collateral damage?"

"Something like that. It was nothing personal He was just in the wrong place at the wrong time. I was sorry when Coach found out about the steroids. But it's business, so he had to go. Tyler was leaving Vitner's house when Pitts showed up. With a little help from Stockade Wade, framing your brother was easy."

"Easy? You ruined his life." A wave of anger overcomes my fear. Slipping my good hand into my coat pocket, I grip the handle of Cece's gun and flick off the safety.

"You've caused me a lot of trouble, Jenna. Stockade Wade was an investment."

"What are you planning to do with me?"

Dylan pulls a pair of black gloves from his pocket. "Never do your own dirty work, unless you're forced. Don't worry. You won't feel much. We'll take you to where Stockade fell through the ice and make it look like he shot you."

Dylan pushes a button, unlocking the car, and Pitts opens my door wide.

"I've been waiting for this," Pitts growls, thrusting his beefy arm toward me.

Before he can grab me, I aim the gun and shoot Pitts straight through my coat. A jagged hole appears in his thigh as the bullet blasts through flesh and hits bone. He screams and stumbles back, falling to the ground with a dazed look on his face. Blood spreads in the snow.

Dylan reaches for the door handle. I point the gun at his head.

"Stop right there. Hands on the wheel."

"Come on, Jenna. We both know you aren't going to shoot me."

"I'm not that high school girl anymore. I *will* take the shot. Now drive."

There's a satisfying level of terror in Dylan's eyes as he accelerates, leaving Roy Pitts bleeding out on the side of the road.

<h1 style="text-align:center">Chapter 25
Closure</h1>

My blood is smeared across the pale leather interior of Dylan's expensive car—something to remember me by, creep. He drives slowly as I check the glove compartment; there's a loaded Glock 19 and a bag stuffed with Happy Kat blotters. I pocket the gun and the drugs. I can't believe I fell for his fake nice guy act.

"You were a dick on our first date," I say, annoyed. "You haven't changed one bit." Then I crack the window open so the cold air keeps me sharp.

"Come on, Jenna," Dylan says. "Stop being so naive." His hands start to slip off the wheel, but I jam the gun in his ribs. A huff of air rushes out of his lungs, and he glares at me.

"Don't try anything," I snap. "Eyes on the road." We fall into a black silence. Every time he slows down, I poke him. The movement sends a jolt of pain up my arm.

A mile before Bell River Police Station, the bars on my phone return.

"Call Cece," I command the electronic assistant and hear the ringback tone.

"Think about what you're doing, Jenna," Dylan pleads.

I ignore him. I know exactly what I'm doing.

"What about us?" He has the audacity to flash his boyish smile.

"Us? That's laughable." I glare at him. What does he think? That I have cotton candy in my head instead of brains?

"Hang up now, and there's a job for you," he spits out in a panic.

"What kind of job?" I ask coolly, toying with him.

"Head of security. A million a year. How does that sound?"

"Let me get this straight…you're offering me a million dollars a year to keep you and your drug business safe?" I laugh, but the sound is cold and hard.

"Jenna? Is that you?" Cece's voice bursts through the phone speaker. "Where have you been?"

"I had some trouble," I say through gritted teeth. "Stockade Wade ran me off the road."

"Damn it! Are you with him?" Cece says.

"Wade fell through the ice over by the Winter Bridge. I'm pretty sure he's dead. And I shot Roy Pitts. He's bleeding out by marker twenty-seven."

"Christ Almighty," Cece says. "That's a lot."

"Listen, I'm coming to the station now—with a suspect."

"A suspect?" she says, confused. "Who?"

"Dylan Connor. He just tried to kill me. Then he tried to bribe me. He's at the center of this whole mess." The line crackles.

"Okay, be careful. I'll see you outside," Cece says. "Tell Dylan not to try anything."

I hang up. "You hear that, Connor?"

"You're missing an opportunity." Dylan eyes the door handle.

"Don't think I won't shoot you. I've had plenty of practice. Hands back on the wheel."

He places both hands where I can see them.

"If you take me in, Jenna, my lawyer will contradict everything you say, delay, argue, call character witnesses... It'll be your word against mine. It'd be smarter to take the money."

"Do you want to do all that with or without your kidneys?" I jab the gun in his side.

Dylan's jaw tightens. "With my kidneys."

"Good. Now, take the turn nice and slow."

We pull into Bell River Police Station. Cece is waiting in the parking lot, arms folded. Officer Pete stands beside her. Maggie peeks from the doorway on tiptoe, trying to see what's happening.

After rolling to a stop, Dylan turns to me. "Damn it, Jenna. There's still time. I was serious about the job, about us—"

I hold my hand up to silence him. As I take a last look at Dylan Connor, his facade seems to dissolve. The warm smile looks more like a car salesman's fake grin. And how did I miss those predatory eyes?

"You think I care whether you're serious? I may not have the best boundaries, Dylan, but I draw the line at a guy who tries to murder me."

Pete yanks the door open and hauls Dylan out of the driver's seat.

"You have the right to remain silent..." he says, cuffing Dylan roughly.

"What are you arresting me for?" Dylan grimaces.

"Murder for hire, to start," I say. "He had Pitts kill Coach Vitner. Oh, and the attempted murder of yours truly." I take a picture of Dylan, then text it to Cole Braedon with the caption: *Meet the Happy Kat kingpin, your pal Dylan Connor.*

Dylan squirms. "I want to talk to my lawyer."

"Book him," Cece says. "Then give him his damned phone call." She turns to me. "Well done, Jenna. Are you alright?"

"Fine." I grin with satisfaction. "I just need a change of clothes."

She examines my arm. "And a trip to the hospital."

Cece's right. I should get my wounds cleaned up, but I want to know what's happening before I leave. "What about the rest of them?"

"I put an APB out on Pitts, Woody, and the Spar brothers," she says. "Search and Rescue is looking for Sheriff Wade." As usual, Cece is on top of things.

"Jenna!" Maggie runs down the steps and squeezes me tight, sending a shooting pain through my arm. "What happened?"

"Ruined my coat," I say and hug her.

Chapter 26
Moving Day

A lot can change in twenty-four hours. That's how long it took for the first TV news crew to show up, for Roy Pitts to confess to killing Coach Vitner, and for Cece to arrest the Spar brothers and Woody Wade. Twenty-four hours later, Woody resigned from his congressional run.

Unfortunately, Tyler's release took longer. Mom and Star visited him regularly, keeping him informed, while Cece, Maggie, and I pulled all-nighters, checking and double-checking the evidence. We documented how Woody and Dylan imported steroids and distributed them through Woody's cousins, the Spar brothers, via their mailbox system. We also discovered (with some help from Cole Braedon) how Dylan's criminal enterprise drew the interest of the Izar Cartel, which was slowly expanding into New York. The two operations built a profitable relationship, pushing street drugs upstate through Dylan's network. Then, when the cartel wanted to test the market for designer drugs, they arranged for Karl Haben, an international criminal chemist, to take a job at the forensics lab where he could synthesize drugs from inside law enforcement. The only thing Dylan didn't count on was Coach Vitner finding his football players pumped up on steroids and caring deeply. When Vitner confronted the Spar brothers, he unwittingly set off his own murder. Dylan hired Roy Pitts as a hitman and set up Tyler to take the fall. Thinking they were in the clear, Haben perfected the Happy Kat formula. The Izar Cartel, with Dylan's help, released the drug into the market.

I still have questions. Was Stockade Wade involved from the start? Or, after Abby's tragic death, was he willing to do anything to protect his only remaining child? We may never know. Woody Wade and Dylan Connor lawyered up, so they aren't talking. We don't even have Sheriff Wade's body. The search was called off until Bell River thaws. There was no inquest into his death; my testimony was considered accurate.

Since my rude awakening—that I almost fell for a criminal psycho who framed my brother—Bell River has been in the news.

"Martha! Turn on the TV!" Mrs. Dupont habitually yells before thundering out her front door and into Mom's house, declaring. "See? I told you. You can't trust anyone, not even the police."

As details emerged, our case merged with Cole Braedon's, and the Feds pressed charges.

Finally, Cece and I documented enough evidence for the Eastmoor County prosecutor to file a motion to vacate Tyler's conviction. Last week, he confided another trial was doubtful, which brings us to my news. A judge in Albany just ordered Ty's release on bond—today is the day.

Cece pulls her Volvo station wagon up to the Eastmoor release gate and shuts off the engine. The gate is about twenty feet away, painted industrial green. I'm riding in the passenger seat with Martha and Star in the back. They're both nervous. It's funny how alike they are...I never saw it before. Both of them are sweet, positive, and caring, both love to thrift shop and bake. I am definitely the black sheep in this extended family.

"I'll just be a second," Cece says. I hand her the paperwork file. She tucks it under one arm and heads for the guard's entrance.

I glance at Mom and Star in the backseat.

Star spent an hour perfecting her makeup and nervously changing her outfit. Loose curls and hoop earrings frame her heart-shaped face. Her cheeks are flushed pink with excitement. She's wearing faded jeans and a floaty, bell-sleeved sweater that looks like fairies spun it on a magical loom. These days, she looks more like her old self and seems comfortable in her skin. She giggles with excitement.

Martha, on the other hand, is strangely quiet. She's wearing a classic cardigan, tan slacks, and the same stoic expression I've grown accustomed to all these years. But something has changed. There's the wisp of a hopeful smile at the corners of her mouth.

"It's really happening, isn't it, Jenna Bean?" Martha whispers.

"Yes, it is." I swallow hard. "We did it."

"You did it," she says, looking at me with gratitude. "My brave, brave girl."

Martha takes Star's hand and squeezes.

I'm going to miss them. I'll be leaving next week, heading back to my life in New York. Knowing that Martha and Star will be there for Tyler, and each other, reassures me.

Then the metal security door creaks and opens. We watch Tyler step out, blink in the sunlight, and smile. He's all corded muscle, his hair is long, and there's a strength in him that wasn't there before.

Cece and Tyler shake hands, before Tyler pulls her in for a hug. With that, Martha can't hold back another second. She steps out onto the pavement.

"Ty! Honey!" she shouts, waving frantically.

"Mom!" He runs into her arms.

"Oh, Tyler." Martha closes her eyes, ruffles his hair, and rocks him.

Star steps out shyly, waiting her turn. I can feel the electricity when their eyes meet. Tyler walks over and tenderly brushes a strand of hair off her face. Then he gathers her into his arms. They hug, and Tyler is so gentle. Then he picks her up off her feet and spins her around. Star breaks into giggles of happiness.

I let them have their moment before I step out of the car—my turn.

Tyler walks over and grabs my shoulders. He looks me in the eyes. We both feel the intensity of what this means.

"I-I never let myself believe you'd get me out," Tyler says, his voice breaking. "But you did, sis. Thank you." Then he hugs me in a bone-crushing grip; it feels like the opposite of getting your heart broken. It feels like love and life and triumph.

"Anything for you, Ty," I say, reveling in the warmth of his presence.

"Home?" He gestures to Cece's wagon.

"If you're sure you're ready," I say. "You know, moving is one of the most stressful things a person can do."

We both burst out laughing before climbing into the car.

Finally, my baby brother is a free man.

Chapter 27
Cheers

As the train pulls into Bell River Station, the sun shines, and a hawk glides across the clear blue sky. The winter snow is long gone, and the sugar maples around the platform are green. The train slows to a stop with a loud hiss. It's hard to believe my internship was only seven months ago.

So much has changed.

"I love the countryside, don't you?" Dave pulls our bags down from the overhead compartment. "The last time I was here, this station looked like an Arctic horror movie."

"Ouch, don't remind me." I double-check my shoulder bag.

"Sure you're ready?" Dave says lightly as he puts on a crisp straw fedora. He's dressed in a white linen suit, ready for a summer soiree. Of course, traveling with Dave is like having a personal stylist. He convinced me to wear a clingy, lavender jersey sundress and a tailored jacket with the sleeves pushed up. I hoist my overnight bag over one shoulder.

"I'm actually looking forward to seeing everyone." I give him a reassuring smile.

"I guess our late-night talks are helping." Dave offers me his hand. We step onto the platform in the bright sunlight. I'm about to call Bell River's only Uber driver, Andy Barnes, when I hear a familiar voice.

"Need a lift?" Detective Cece Myers leans against the platform railing, dressed casually in jeans, a white T-shirt, and a bomber jacket.

I run over and throw my arms around her. "You just cheated Andy Barnes out of a fare."

"He's downing mimosas at your mom's shindig. I thought I'd better get you myself."

"And who is this vision?" Dave says. Impossible as it seems, the two have never met.

"Detective Cece Myers, meet my best friend, Dave."

Cece offers her hand formally. But her smile is warm.

"Supercop Cece?" He ignores her hand and kisses both her cheeks. "Enchanté."

"Another Francophile? You and my husband are going to get along great." Cece grins sheepishly. Not even she can resist Dave's charm.

We climb into Cece's Volvo and head toward town. As we follow the main road, the grass pushes up, and the wildflowers bloom. The place feels different, more innocent.

"Did you hear Maggie got promoted?" Cece says. "She'll run the refurbished Bell River Crime Lab soon."

"How perfect is that? I can see the Post-It notes from here."

Cece laughs, and it's a nice sound.

"Aren't you gunning for a new job too?" Dave teases.

"Guilty as charged," Cece says. "I'm hoping to be elected Sheriff of this fine county."

"Martha tells me you're a shoo-in," I say.

"Well, let's hope so. Boomer loves this town."

"Do you?" Dave leans in from the back seat.

"You know..." Cece pauses. "I do. Bell River finally feels like home."

As we approach the Winter Bridge, I'm struck by the lush landscape. The crowns of the red oaks have filled out, the river has thawed, and the cattails bloom. I lower my window. Birds chirp in the trees, and a rabbit scampers into the brush. Passing over the river, there's no sign of danger, just slow-moving water reflecting the summer sun. I flash on the horrible moment Stockade Wade fell through the ice. Search and Rescue never found his body. I wonder if they ever will.

"How about some music?" Cece turns on a classic rock station. I'm grateful for the distraction, and we fall into a comfortable silence the rest of the way into town.

As Cece turns the Volvo onto 4th Street, something about downtown has changed. I try to pinpoint what it is exactly. Things look cleaner, the trees are trimmed, and the alleyways are trash-free. The cracked windows along the street are gone.

Up ahead, a sandwich board with Welcome to Martha's Mementos painted in pink cursive writing marks the spot. Cece glides into a parking space. Dozens of guests spill onto the sidewalk, holding champagne glasses. The enormous Craftsman-style building once housed a popular bookstore, but the beautiful old structure sat empty and neglected for years. The exterior has been refurbished with freshly sanded and stained wood. This loving restoration is just one example of how Tyler's settlement with Eastmoor County has changed lives. He could have pushed for more money, but he's more like our mom than I am. He just wanted to forgive and move on. But he still walked away with several million dollars. Between Tyler's investment and Mom's vision, her antique shop officially opens today.

"Look at this place," Dave says as he steps onto the sidewalk.

"It's like Martha Stewart and Bilbo Baggins had a baby. So quaint. Ooh, and it looks like there's an open bar." Dave air-kisses my cheeks and disappears through the front door.

"See you inside," Cece says and squeezes my arm before going to find Boomer.

"Jenna!" Maggie waves at me, wearing a black baby-doll dress and wedge sandals. Her blue pompom ponytails are now pink. Shane stands next to her in plaid shorts and a *Jaws* T-shirt.

"Magpie!" I make my way to them and hug her tightly. "Congratulations."

"You heard?" She beams with joy.

"Cece told me."

"How did Cece know?" She looks confused. "We just got engaged last night." Maggie holds out her hand, showing me a delicate gold ring shaped like vines sprinkled with tiny diamonds.

"Cece told me about your promotion. But crime lab boss and a wedding? I'm so happy for you both."

"Thanks, Jenna." Shane puts his arm around Maggie. "We're thinking about a winter wedding with sleighs, maybe a fairy theme."

"I—I mean, we," says Maggie, "would love you to be Maid of Honor."

"Me? That would be incredible."

Shane pulls us into a three-way hug. With all of the danger and terrible revelations, Maggie and Shane's relationship is one of the best things to come out of our investigation.

"Jenna Bean!" Martha appears at the doorway waving.

"Go!" Maggie says. "We'll talk dresses later."

"Welcome to my dream come true," Mom announces as she leads me into Martha's Mementos. The store is crammed with well-wishers sipping champagne and marveling at the many treasures on display. Everyone is smiling, chatting, and milling between rooms. A sturdy oak desk for ringing and wrapping purchases is inside the front door. Annie Dupont is stationed there, wearing a crisp, white apron with Martha's Mementos embroidered in pink.

"Mrs. Dupont! Hello."

Annie looks at her watch and scowls. "The party started an hour ago, Missy."

"Now, Annie. Remember our motto?" Martha says softly.

"Every customer is our future friend," Annie recites painfully.

"Don't let her bother you," Mom says, leading me away. "She's been wonderful. I never could have done this without her."

"Annie Dupont works for you?"

"Well, yes. But I like to say she's helping out. She's a very proud woman, you know. But she's such a hard worker and knows her history and antiques."

Mom leads me from room to room, each set up with a theme. The kitchen has displays of fine china, vintage linens, and silver, alongside period tea sets and salt and pepper shakers. The living room is stuffed with antique furniture, bar carts, and lamps, with an old Victrola set up in the corner.

At the end of the hall is a door marked *Study*. I expect a library full of dusty old books or an office. Instead, we enter a bright, cheerful room with stacks of writing supplies. Three brand-new computers are stationed on a large table surrounded by comfortable chairs. A window with gingham curtains tied back with ribbons overlooks the street.

"What's this?" I run my hand over a chenille throw pillow.

"It's the study, dear." She points to the sign. "Children can come by for free tutoring or just a cozy place to do their homework and have a snack."

My eyes well up. Of course, she included a space for the kids. If anyone on earth deserves their dream, it's my mom.

"Martha? There you are. I've been looking for you." Emma Downing, president of The Bell River Historical Society, stands in the doorway, hands on her hips, wearing a bright yellow suit with frosted hair. She reminds me of an angry baby chick.

"Emma, so nice to see you," Mom says politely. "Can I help you with something?"

"Annie said you're planning to host an antique fair?"

"Well, yes. It's still in its infancy, but we thought some commerce and tourism could do wonders for the town."

I brace myself for a rude remark from Mrs. Downing.

But instead of a condescending put-down, she smiles.

"I think it's a wonderful idea." Emma claps her hands. "Perhaps the Historical Society could get involved and sponsor some activities?"

Wow. Annie Dupont works for Martha, and Emma Downing is trying to ride her coattails? Things sure have changed around here.

"That's very generous, Emma. We'll be sure to reach out." Mom brushes past her. "Right now, I'm showing my daughter around."

"Of course. Nice to see you, Jenna."

I follow Mom to our last unexplored room downstairs, staged like a dining room and bustling with activity. Luscious baked goods—scones, cookies, brownies, and cupcakes—cover every surface, displayed on paper doilies. The heady aroma of sugar and butter fills the air. A sideboard holds iced and hot tea, orange juice, and champagne. Visitors fill delicate, mismatched plates with goodies and use linen napkins—no plastic or paper for Martha's guests.

"How did you have time to make all of this?" I marvel.

Martha smiles and looks past me. "I had help."

I follow her gaze to Audrey Vitner. She has frosting on her nose, and her Martha's Mementos apron is covered with flour. In her hands is a cake. She holds the plate out to show me. Written in red letters on snowy white icing are the words: *Thank you, Jenna.*

"I told you I'd bake you a cake." Audrey sets the dessert down and cuts me a slice. The inside is a deep crimson. "When you first stopped by, I thought, how is this inexperienced, headstrong girl going to find out what happened to my Joe?" she says with a steely calm. "But you surprised us all." Audrey hands me the slice of cake. "So, I wanted to keep my promise."

I taste a forkful of cake. The flavor is rich and buttery, with a deep cocoa undertone. It's delicious.

"Red velvet. My favorite."

"Shall we bring the rest outside?" Mom suggests loading the cake, plates, and forks onto a silver tray. "I think your brother's out there."

I follow Mom to the back patio. The yard has outdoor furniture, a tasteful fountain, and sculptures with vines growing over the stonework. Tyler and Star are sitting in a loose group with Dave, Boomer, and Cece. A lanky guy with dark hair has his back to me. He must be hilarious from the way they're all laughing.

"Où dimanche vient-il avant jeudi?" the man says in perfect French.

"Je ne sais pas, pourquoi?" Boomer says, nudging Tyler.

"Dans le dictionnaire?" Tyler says.

"Oh my gosh." Dave claps his hands in delight. "Where does Sunday come before Thursday? In the dictionary!"

"Bien joué," the man says.

Tyler spots me and waves me over. "Jenna! Come meet my friend."

Boomer slides his chair over to make room. They've gotten very friendly since Ty's been helping out at the Bistro. When Boomer heard he wanted to be a chef, he took Tyler under his wing. Star is nestled next to Ty and waves happily, her long hair draped over her shoulders.

"Bonjour les amis," I greet them in French.

The guy with dark hair turns around. His green eyes are only too familiar.

Cole Braedon grins up at me. "Bonjour beauté."

"Cole? W-what are you doing here?" My stomach flutters in surprise, or excitement, or both. He's the last person I expected to see today.

"Tyler invited me. Didn't you, buddy?"

"Tyler?" I look at my brother, who nods.

"I'd only been working at the bistro for a month when this guy comes in and orders a Truffle Soufflé. Boomer insisted I prepare the dish. I was sweating bullets, let me tell you. Luckily, the soufflé turned out perfectly, and I met Cole when he asked to compliment the chef."

"What can I say? I've had some downtime," Cole says. "And I can't resist Boomer's food."

Dave has a strange look on his face. He stares at Cole, and his eyes glow brightly with realization. Then he looks at me knowingly.

"Did you say Cole Braedon?" Dave leans in with interest. "As in *the* Cole Braedon?"

"Why? Has Jenna mentioned me?" Cole smiles with a level of confidence that should be illegal.

"You could say that..." Dave glances at me. "I think she mentioned a road trip—"

"Nobody wants to hear about that." I shake my head slowly, emphasizing the *No*.

Cece stares at Cole Braedon with the trained eye of a detective.

"Where are you from, Cole?" she asks flatly.

"Different places." He grins. "Here and there."

"Are you Jenna's anonymous contact?"

"Me? I just like to help Jenna now and then."

Dave sips his mimosa with a grin that can only be described as the cat who ate the canary. He knows everything, of course... all the strange, frustrating, and sexy exchanges between Cole and me. But he's the only one who does know. Despite Cole supplying evidence in the case, Tyler never met him. And despite Cece knowing I have a source at the FBI, she has no idea who my contact was. And to me, Cole is just an existential black hole of questions I can't answer and emotions I can't afford to indulge.

"Cole brings the wine, and we practice our French," Boomer says. "His French is better than mine. He speaks like a native."

"That's how Cole and Boomer convinced me to go to Le Cordon Bleu. My term starts in September and lasts for six months." Tyler takes Star's hand. "So we leave in August."

"I've never been to Paris," Star says, excited. "We want to spend time together before I start my master's in communication at SUNY New Paltz."

"And when Ty gets back, he's got a place with me," Boomer says. "If he wants."

Mesmerized, I start to sit down next to Star, but Cole circles my wrist and guides me to the seat next to him. Then he immediately starts eating the cake off my plate.

"What's going on here, Braedon?" I eye him suspiciously.

He smiles wickedly. "Red velvet's my favorite."

"Seriously." I'm happy to see him, but an antique store grand opening is hardly his speed. I lean in and whisper in a low voice. "Why are you really here?"

He shrugs and glances at Tyler. "It can be a tough adjustment," he says softly, then louder. "We're working out tomorrow, right, Ty?"

Suddenly, I understand. Cole's been to prison, too. He's been checking in on my brother.

There are no words to express my gratitude to this strange, mysterious man who fed me evidence, guided me, and believed in Tyler almost as much as I did.

"Thank you," I whisper and squeeze his arm. "I don't know what—"

"I'd do anything for you, Jenna. Don't you know that by now?" This time, when Cole looks at me, it's as if the rest of the world doesn't exist.

But the everyday world does exist—the realm of school, work, and unglamorous responsibilities. Would Cole ever fit into that world? I doubt it.

Before I can answer him, Martha steps out onto the patio and taps her glass with a knife.

"Excuse me. Can I have your attention, please?"

Everyone looks her way, and people migrate to the garden. Maggie and Shane step outside, holding hands. The murmuring of conversation quiets down.

"I wanted to thank you for coming to celebrate the opening of Martha's Mementos. Special thanks to Tyler, Annie, Star, and Audrey for helping put this wonderful party together. But today is so much more than a shop-warming party. It's proof that a community can come together—that hard work, love, and sheer stubbornness" —she smiles at me with pride— "can defeat evil and corruption. That a town isn't defined by its history. We make our own story. I love this town. Here's to you—to all of us. To Bell River." She raises her glass. "To the future."

"To the future!" the crowd responds.

I look around the table at these people I love. With all the crazy things that have happened, I feel so grateful to have family and friends I can count on. Dave's lip is trembling, and he dabs at the corner of his eyes with one of Martha's fancy napkins. Star rests her head on Tyler's shoulder.

Not surprisingly, Cole slipped out during Mom's speech. But maybe he's found some camaraderie in Bell River. I hope so.

Cece catches my eye from across the table. "What about you, Jenna? I hear you're graduating?"

"With honors, thanks to you, boss."

"Then what?" Boomer says.

"I start a job at a private investigations firm in the fall. Maybe I can help some families like ours get justice."

"Cheers to that." Tyler polishes off his champagne.

Cece smiles and holds up her glass. "Just remember, this town has a warm heart despite the cold winters. There's always a place for you here in Bell River."

About Hanna Wren

Books by Hanna Wren
The Deadliest Lead
A Dangerous Favor
The Bell River Murder

About Hanna Wren
Hanna Wren is the pen name authors Amy Eyrie and Alix Sloan use when writing together. Visit HannaWren.com to learn more about them, find Hanna Wren on social media, and join the Hanna Wren mailing list.

Thank You!
Thank you for reading *The Bell River Murder*. We hope you enjoyed it! If you did, please consider leaving a short review. We'd be very grateful, as reviews play a vital role in helping new readers discover our books.